"Let's go!" Billy signaled.

And he led the band out onto the Roadhouse's oversized stage.

As soon as the band came onto the stage, a bank of spotlights flashed, red and blue lasers danced crazily, and the sound of a bass drum—recorded, because Jake hadn't even gotten behind his drum kit—filled the air.

Emma got that familiar rush of excitement—the one she hadn't ever known before she joined the band, but which she now recognized from every single time she'd been onstage with them.

But something's wrong, *Emma realized as she took her place at the backup singers' mike, blinded temporarily by the spotlights.* There's something completely wrong here.

And then she realized what it was.

It's silent out there, *she thought.* Usually everyone's yelling and screaming. But I don't hear a single voice from the crowd!

The SUNSET ISLAND series
by Cherie Bennett

Sunset Island
Sunset Kiss
Sunset Dreams
Sunset Farewell
Sunset Reunion
Sunset Secrets
Sunset Heat
Sunset Promises
Sunset Scandal
Sunset Whispers
Sunset Paradise
Sunset Surf
Sunset Deceptions
Sunset on the Road
Sunset Embrace
Sunset Wishes
Sunset Touch
Sunset Wedding
Sunset Glitter
Sunset Stranger
Sunset Heart
Sunset Revenge
Sunset Sensation
Sunset Magic
Sunset Illusions
Sunset Fire
Sunset Fantasy
Sunset Passion
Sunset Love
Sunset Fling
Sunset Tears
Sunset Spirit

The CLUB SUNSET ISLAND series
by Cherie Bennett

Too Many Boys!
Dixie's First Kiss
Tori's Crush

Also created by Cherie Bennett

Sunset After Dark
Sunset After Midnight
Sunset After Hours

Sunset Spirit

CHERIE BENNETT

Sunset™ Island

SPLASH™

A BERKLEY / SPLASH BOOK

SUNSET SPIRIT is an original publication of
The Berkley Publishing Group.
This work has never appeared before in book form.

SUNSET SPIRIT

A Berkley Book / published by arrangement with
General Licensing Company, Inc.

PRINTING HISTORY
Berkley edition / September 1995

For information address: General Licensing Company, Inc.,
24 West 25th Street, New York, New York 10010.

A GLC BOOK

ISBN: 0-425-15028-3

BERKLEY®
Berkley Books are published by
The Berkley Publishing Group,
200 Madison Avenue, New York, New York 10016.

PRINTED IN THE UNITED STATES OF AMERICA

10 9 8 7 6 5 4 3 2 1

For J.G., forever.

ONE

Emma Cresswell sighed, picked up her pen, and began to write.

Dear Diary,

Okay. I'll tell the truth. Tonight I came as close to being ready to marry Kurt again as I've ever been.

We had the most wonderful evening. He picked me up in his taxi when I was finished with work at the Hewitts' house, and we drove to a secret spot he knew on the bay side of the island. Since Kurt grew up here on Sunset Island, he knows all these great places. . . .

She stopped a moment and glanced at the clock. Midnight. She wasn't at all tired.

Instead of trying to sleep, which she knew would be futile, she turned back to the tapestry-covered diary her aunt Liz had given her when she first came to Sunset Island.

It seems like a lifetime ago, she thought, nibbling at the end of her pen. *Once I started to work as an au pair on this island, my entire life changed. I went from being a spoiled rich girl to having my first job, my first true best friends, and my first love. . . .*

Kurt. I love him so much. And we've been through so much together. To think I almost lost him . . .

She got more comfortable on her bed and put her pen back to the paper.

> It was the most incredibly romantic night. There were no boats on the bay at all, just a lone seabird that kept circling in the air high above the water. Kurt had brought a blanket with him, and we were totally secluded. I couldn't see anything but the bay, and Kurt, and no one could see us.

We talked for a while, mostly about my mother and his father, and then he took me in his arms and kissed me. When I opened my eyes after that first delicious kiss, I could see him looking at me.

Emma looked up from her diary and out the window of her small room on the top floor of Jeff and Jane Hewitt's house, where she lived for the summer, and where she was employed to care for the Hewitts' three children, Ethan, Wills, and little Katie. The room was illuminated by the rays of the full moon. And as she gazed outside she could see herself and Kurt just a couple of hours before.

I felt ready to let myself go to him completely, again, emotionally. But in other ways I knew I was still holding back. How can it be that I have all these feelings for him, but still, in some ways, I don't feel ready? I can't tell anyone this. I can only write it here. But it felt so wonderful to be in his arms!

Emma put her pen down again and looked back out the bedroom window, back to the smiling face of the man in the moon.

I suppose some people would tell me I'm crazy, or hopeless, she thought. *After all, I'm nineteen years old. Can't I just get over it?*

She sighed and put her head down on her hands. *Well, at least my friends are with me in this,* she thought. *Sam's still holding back with Pres, I think. She says we two are probably the oldest virgins in America. As for Carrie, she's the most mature, together girl I've ever known, and she and Billy are in a long-term, totally committed relationship. I'm sure they'll be together forever.*

Her mind drifted back to the incredible sequence of events that had brought her to Sunset Island, and had led her, Carrie Alden, and Samantha Bridges to had become best friends.

We're all so different from each other,

Emma thought. *I'm from a really rich Boston family—okay, Sam would call it mega-rich!—and she always teases me because I'm petite and blond and I wear clothes that are kind of classic. Sam, meanwhile, was raised in Kansas—she even had a pet pig when she was little—and is tall and thin with lots of red hair. And she is wild! She has the greatest sense of style; I wish I had the courage to wear what she wears.*

And Carrie. Carrie's the most level-headed girl I've ever met. Her parents are both doctors in New Jersey, and she's going to Yale. Even though she thinks she needs to lose weight, I think she looks great. She dresses in baggy clothes most of the time, but Sam says that she'd kill to have Carrie's bustline!

The three girls had all met at the International Au Pair Convention in New York City more than a year before, and had become fast friends. Emma still didn't know what had gotten into her that made her want to become an au pair for the summer after she'd finished high school.

But she'd done it, and she'd been hired to work for the Hewitt family on fabulous Sunset Island, the world-famous resort island off the coast of Maine, at the far reaches of Casco Bay. Then, to her amazement, Sam and Carrie had been hired by families who spent their summers on the island, too.

Carrie works for Graham Perry, the rock star, and his family, Emma thought. *And she doesn't even like rock music that much! Sam has offered to trade employers with her a million times, since she works for Dan Jacobs, who's a little bit like a kid himself, and his twin fourteen-year-old daughters, Allie and Becky, who think they're already over twenty-one!*

And now we're back on the island again for our second summer. I never want it to come to an end. But it's going to, practically before I know it, and then I'm going to go back to Goucher College, and Kurt's going into the Air Force Academy, and then . . .

"Then what?" Emma whispered out loud.

She rolled over onto her back and stared at the ceiling.

My mother hates Kurt, she thought. *In fact, she even cut me off financially just because I wouldn't stop seeing him! It's not his fault if he's from a poor family and he grew up right here on the island. He's going to make something wonderful of his life, and my mother is a narrow-minded snob.*

She rolled over again and pondered her open diary. *How can I sort out all my feelings?* she wondered. *I'm so mixed up. I love Kurt more than anything, but I hate having no money. And I want to be with him forever, but I also want to go back to college, and join the Peace Corps, and . . . well, do a million things! But what if that means I lose him?*

She thought about writing some more, then changed her mind and put the diary on the nightstand. *I know one thing for sure,* she thought as she crawled under the covers. *I'm not going to get in as far emotionally as I was before until I'm ready to make it forever.*

Even if that means you'll lose him? a voice in her head asked her.

"If Kurt really loves me, it won't matter,"

she said out loud as she punched her pillow into a better position.

Even though your archenemy, Diana De Witt, had a hot fling with him? the same evil voice asked inside Emma's head.

"Shut up!" she told the voice crossly. "That was a long time ago. He made a mistake. That's all."

But even as she drifted off to sleep she couldn't get the image of Diana wrapped in Kurt's arms out of her mind.

"Good morning, Emma," Jane Hewitt said as Emma came into the Hewitts' kitchen the next morning.

"Morning," Emma replied, going to the stove to fix herself her usual cup of tea. She was in a much better mood than she'd been in the night before, when she'd been unable to sleep.

The sun is shining, I'm young, and I'm in love, she reminded herself. *Plus the Flirts' tour is coming up, and it's going to be incredible. Kurt and I will be together for four whole days, because he's going along as road manager!*

Emma and Sam were both backup singers with the Flirts, as the band Flirting With Danger was known locally. Started by Carrie's boyfriend, Billy Sampson, and featuring Sam's on-again, off-again boyfriend, Presley Travis, the group was extremely well known in southern Maine.

Now the Flirts were going to start a short four-day tour of Maine—with stops in Bangor, Waterville, Lewiston, and Portland—that was supposed to allow Polimar Records, the big record label, to decide whether to sign the band to a recording contract.

Polimar had been considering signing the Flirts for almost a year. This tour was going to be the moment of truth. A Polimar executive was going to accompany them to every stop on the tour. They'd either get the deal or have to look elsewhere.

Emma smiled at the Hewitt family, who were all sitting around the breakfast table. There was four-year-old Katie, who had a pair of swim goggles dangling around her neck as she sat happily munching on some dry breakfast cereal, seven-year-old Wills, their twelve-year-old brother, Ethan, and their father, Jeff Hewitt. Jane and Jeff were both lawyers.

And they're also the most wonderful adults I've ever met in my life, Emma thought as she poured boiling water into her cup. *I only wish my mother was more like Jane!*

"I'm ready for the club!" Katie chirped happily, swinging her legs under the kitchen table. "Kwatic Kapers today!"

The Kwatic Kapers, Emma knew, was a sort of low-level swimming contest for the youngest kids at the Sunset Country Club. Katie was too young for Club Sunset Island, the day camp at the club, but the swimming instructors there occasionally organized various activities for the younger kids. In the Kwatic Kapers, kids did things such as find coins that were at the bottom of the kiddie pool.

"I'm a big monster!" Katie cried in a spooky voice as she put the oversized swim goggles on.

"Gag me," Wills mumbled, reaching for his orange juice.

"I'm a monster and I'm going to eat you!" Katie said, reaching for her brother.

"I'm not on the menu," Wills replied with dignity.

Emma glanced over at Jeff, who was uncharacteristically dressed in a business suit, crisp white shirt, and bright yellow-and-black polka-dot tie instead of his usual summer vacation clothes.

"You look nice," Emma told him.

Jeff smiled at her. "You're wondering about the suit, huh?"

"A little," Emma admitted, stirring some honey into her tea.

"I got a call from Miami this morning," Jeff related, taking a quick glance at his watch. "My case was called for tomorrow morning."

Emma looked at him quizzically, not comprehending what he was saying.

"His case," Jane Hewitt explained. "Jeff's trying a product-liability lawsuit in the Miami federal district court. Something about paint remover."

"My client claimed the fumes gave him a heart attack. I've been waiting two years to get to trial," Jeff continued, shaking his head ruefully. "And now they give me a day's notice to get down there!"

"He's got a ten o'clock flight from Portland," Jane said. "I'm taking him to the airport."

"I'll miss you guys," Jeff said.

"In Miami?" Ethan said. "I don't think so!"

"How come?" Katie asked her brother.

"Miami is a party city," Ethan said. "Right, Dad?"

"Your father parties only with me, dear," Jane said with a grin.

"That's right," Jeff replied, a twinkle glinting in his brown eyes.

"It better be right," Jane joshed. "You're not the only lawyer in this house!"

"Daddy, do you have to go?" Katie whined, climbing into her father's lap.

"Yes, honey," Jeff said, giving his daughter a hug, swim goggles and all. "But I'll call every night."

"Daddy will be working hard," Jane said gently, trying to soothe the girl's feelings.

"When will you be back?" Emma asked him.

"In about two weeks," Jeff said, finishing his coffee. He and his wife traded a look.

Emma froze, her teacup halfway to her lips.

Did he say he would be away for two weeks? she asked herself. *Because if he did . . .*

Jeff turned to Emma and shrugged apologetically. "I'm sorry, Emma," he said. "I can't control the judicial calendar. The judge sets the docket, I go. That's just the way it is."

Emma gulped hard. "Are you saying . . . what I think you're saying?"

Jane nodded reluctantly. "The Flirts are going to have to manage without you. We're sorry, Emma. But your job here comes first. I'm going to need you."

"I understand," Emma said faintly, but her mind was racing a million miles a minute.

"We're really sorry, Emma," Jeff added, "but there's really nothing I can do."

"I'm going to have my hands full," Jane

agreed. "I know it's a disappointment to you. But I'm sure you can see the problem."

"Bummer," Ethan commented.

"Bummer," his little sister echoed.

"Bummer," Wills added.

No kidding. Bummer, Emma said to herself. *How can I ever face the band again? They're counting on me!*

"I know it seems terrible," Jane said, taking a sip of her coffee. "But when we agreed to give you the time off, we told you that if something came up, you'd have to stay here."

"And unfortunately something's come up," Jeff stated. He got up from the breakfast table. "Excuse me. I've got some work to do at the computer before I go." He left the kitchen and went into the small home office that Jane and Jeff kept in their summer house.

"I'm sorry," Jane repeated. "I just wish there were something I could do."

"I can take care of Wills and Katie," Ethan offered helpfully.

"I'm afraid not," Jane said.

"I'm old enough," Ethan insisted. "The Flirts need Emma!"

"He's old enough," Katie chimed in. Emma smiled at the little girl, despite her predicament.

"You are not old enough," Wills said. "I wouldn't listen to you if my life depended on it."

"Me neither," Katie agreed, changing her mind capriciously and folding her hands. She stuck her tongue out at her brother.

Do I really want children someday? Emma thought with an inward chuckle, momentarily forgetting her situation.

"Hey, chill out, okay?" Jane suggested to her kids mildly.

Oh my God, Emma thought, her mind returning to the Flirts' tour. *What in the world am I going to do?*

TWO

"Oh, no!" Carrie exclaimed when Emma told her the news. "What are you going to do?"

"I haven't the faintest idea," Emma admitted as she reached down to spread some more sunscreen on her legs.

It was later that morning—nearly noon, in fact. Sam, Emma, and Carrie were all at the country club. Emma and Carrie were keeping an eye on Katie Hewitt and Chloe Templeton, one of Graham Perry Templeton's two kids. The two small girls were taking part in the Kwatic Kapers, which were in full swing in the kiddie pool.

Sam, on the other hand, wasn't watching anyone. Becky and Allie Jacobs were both counselors-in-training at Club Sunset Island, which meant that Sam basically had her days free.

"But you have to come on the tour!" Sam exclaimed. "Don't Jeff and Jane understand how important this is?"

"They feel terrible," Emma explained. "But they *have* given me a lot of time off this summer so I could sing with the Flirts, and they did tell me that my job with them had to come first."

"But this is our big break!" Sam exploded. "I can't believe they're doing this to you!"

"Hey, it's not Jeff's fault that he has to go try a case," Carrie pointed out.

"So what is the big, bad deal if Jane had to take care of her own kids by herself for four days, huh?" Sam demanded. "Millions of women do it, you know."

A cheer went up from near the kiddie pool, temporarily interrupting the girls' conversation. Chloe Templeton had just won some sort of race that involved filling a plastic soda bottle with pool water using a teaspoon, and then emptying the bottle over the head of another camper.

"They've got the life," Sam noted. "And you've got the pits, Emma."

"I don't think the Flirts are going to be very happy. Especially Billy," Emma agreed.

"That's the understatement of the century," Sam added.

"Don't be too hard on yourself," Carrie said reasonably, adjusting her sunglasses against the bright Maine summer sun. "Billy'll understand."

"Ha," Sam snorted. "The band is the most important thing in the world to him—well, other than you, Car. Where's he going to find someone to replace Emma on such short notice?"

"And he has to find a soprano," Carrie put in, "since you and Erin are both altos."

Carrie was referring to Erin Kane, a girl they'd all met on the island this summer and who had become the third member of the backup singer trio for the Flirts. Erin was very pretty, with long, curly blond hair. She was really nice and really funny. And she was also at least forty pounds overweight. But that didn't seem to stop her from getting cute guys. Currently she was involved with Jake Fisher, the drummer who'd replaced Sly, the Flirts' original drummer.

"Well, the good news is that it can't be Diana," Sam pointed out. "She isn't a soprano."

Emma turned to Carrie. "Do you think Billy is going to be really upset?"

"He'll be upset, yes," Carrie conceded, "but he'll handle it. It might not be that hard to find a replacement for just this tour."

"Maybe you're right," Emma ventured, taking a sip of the iced tea she'd ordered earlier.

"And maybe she's wrong," Sam offered. "We've been practicing our butts off together lately. And how about this replacement babe having to learn all the dance combinations?"

"Backup singers are backup singers," Carrie said.

"Yeah, but—" Sam began.

"Really, it'll be okay," Carrie said.

"But—"

"On an album there might not even be backups," Carrie said, trying to make things as easy for Emma as she could.

"Time out, time out," Sam called, making a T with her hands. "Are you saying that we are, like, window dressing or something? Unimportant? Expendable?"

"I'm just saying that it's not as if . . . as if Pres broke his arm or something," Carrie said.

Sam sank back into her lounge chair. "Well, it's a major drag, that's all I have to say. And the tour won't be nearly as much fun without you. I'm bummed out."

"Me, too," Emma said softly.

"No, you're not, ice princess," Sam remarked with a grin. "You're disappointed, aggravated, irritated, and unhappy, but Emma Cresswell has never once used the words *bummed out* in her entire life!"

All three girls broke into laughter. Sam had the ability to laugh about anything, anytime, anywhere. It was one of her best qualities.

"Maybe you could at least do the gig in Portland," Sam thought out loud.

"That's the last stop," Carrie recalled. "I'm sure that would work!"

"Maybe I'm giving up too easily," Emma said as another cheer went up from the kiddie pool. The kids were having a competition to see who could make the biggest splash with their hands. One little boy had just splashed water all the way over to the far row of lounge chairs, nearly soaking an older lady there. Katie and Chloe gave each other a high five to celebrate.

"You think those two will be like us when they're our age?" Carrie wondered.

"No one could be as bodacious as we are," Sam quipped.

Carrie laughed. "Do you actually believe half of the things you say?"

"No," Sam admitted, "but they can shove red-hot pokers under my fingernails before I'll admit that to anyone but you guys." She turned to Emma, who had a faraway look on her face. "I can see the wheels turning in your head, girlfriend."

"Maybe we can think of something," Emma mused.

"Like what?" Sam asked.

"I don't know," Emma acknowledged. "Something to get me out of this. Are you two sure you can get the time off yourselves?"

"Piece of cake," Sam said smugly, adjusting one of the straps on the daisy-print bikini she was wearing. "After that fiasco when Dan fired me and the twins got me rehired, I can wrap my employer around my little finger. Dan's promised me the four nights off."

"Same with Graham and Claudia," Carrie told Emma. "It's not a problem."

"I've got to think of something!" Emma cried, pounding her fist into the cushions of her lounge chair. "I really, really want to go!"

"Too bad you can't buy your way—" Sam began to say, but Carrie cut her off.

"Sam," Carrie warned.

"Then again, I guess you're as poor as we are now," Sam said with a shrug. She shook her head. "Your mother is crazy, Em."

"Believe me, I know that," Emma agreed. "Don't get me started on Kat. I'll get even more depressed than I already am."

Emma closed her eyes, and Kat's words came back to her. "All you have to do," Kat had trilled, "is to drop that silly little taxi driver." And no matter how much Emma had remonstrated that Kurt wasn't just a taxi driver, that he was starting at the Air Force Academy in the fall, Kat had dismissed her daughter as being involved in utter folly.

"You're thinking about her, I know it," Sam said, eyeing Emma.

Emma opened her eyes again. "You're right."

"Can your dad help you?" Carrie asked Emma.

Emma shook her head. "Not really," she said. "I've talked to him, and it's not as bad for him financially as it was before, but it's still bad."

"He really got hurt in the stock market

crash, huh?" Sam asked Emma, and Emma nodded.

"Maybe you can clone yourself," Sam suggested whimsically. "You know, a sci-fi kind of thing. One of you can drop Kurt and get your millions back, and the other one can spend every minute with Kurt doing everything our parents always warned us not to do."

Carrie giggled, and even Emma smiled. "Unfortunately I don't think that's possible." Emma sighed as another huge cheer went up from the Kwatic Kapers.

"They're stopping for lunch," Carrie observed as Katie and Chloe both came running over to her and her friends.

"So, I guess you're gonna break the news to the band tonight, huh?" Sam asked Emma. "We've got practice."

"How could I forget?" Emma grimaced.

"Okay," Billy said, unslinging his guitar from around his neck. "Let's take a break."

"We've got cold drinks on ice in the living room," his band partner, Presley Travis, drawled in his Tennessee accent.

The whole band, who'd been rehearsing in the music room at the Flirts' house, dutifully filed into the living room, where, true to Pres's word, there was a huge bucket filled with cans of soda and bottles of beer.

Sam, Erin, and Emma each took a diet soda. Billy and Pres grabbed beers, and Jay Bailey and Jake picked up cans of iced tea.

Usually a Flirts rehearsal was an informal thing, but because this was one of their last practices before the tour, everyone—even Sam—had been dead serious about the music. And Billy had driven them hard. They'd been in the music room for nearly two hours without a break, and the girls were soaking wet from doing their dance routines over and over.

"Hey, when are you going to drop the bombshell?" Sam whispered to Emma as they made their way toward one of the threadbare couches.

"I know I have to do it," Emma agreed with a sigh, "but it's so awful!"

"Tell him now," Sam advised her. "You'd better."

Emma gave a helpless shrug, but she knew Sam was right.

Billy beat her to the punch, though.

"Guys," he said when everyone had settled in, "we've got a problem, and we gotta put our heads together to solve it."

Everyone looked at him quizzically.

"Look," he said, glancing pointedly at Emma, "I hope you don't mind, but Carrie filled me in on your situation, and I told Pres."

"She did?" Emma asked with surprise. "I'm really sorry," she went on. "I should have told you at the beginning of the rehearsal, but I just—"

"Hey, girl, it's okay," Pres interrupted in his Southern drawl. "We know it's a hard thing for you to tell us, and we know it's not your fault."

Emma smiled at him gratefully.

"What's up?" Jay, the keyboard player, asked, folding his arms.

"Here's the deal," Billy said. Then he

outlined what had transpired at the Hewitts' that day.

"Bummer," Jake said, shaking his head.

Emma smiled ruefully. "That's exactly what the kids I take care of said."

"So what do we do?" Jay asked. "I mean, you've worked so hard on the perfect blend of voices, and the dance routines aren't so easy to learn, either!"

"If anyone has any bright ideas," Billy advised them, "let me know."

"We're goin' on the assumption that we're gonna figure something out," Pres said.

"Maybe Jeff Hewitt will lose the case on the first day," Sam joked.

"We've got two options," Billy continued. "We can cut the backups for the tour, or we can replace Emma."

"Please, please, don't let it be Diana," Sam begged.

"Maybe Sam and I could change our vocal parts around a little and we could do the tour with two backups," Erin suggested.

"You think that's possible?" Billy asked, a little skeptically.

Sam nodded eagerly.

Emma gave her a careful look. *Singing harmony lines is Sam's great weakness,* she thought. *If Erin tries to change Sam's vocal lines now, she'll never be able to relearn them in time!*

"Well, I say we postpone a decision on this for a while," Billy said. "You want me to go over the plans for the tour again?"

Everyone nodded. Billy then spent about five minutes talking about their itinerary. They were going to be playing clubs ranging in size from two hundred to a thousand seats—the last being Jack of Clubs, a new rock and roll club in downtown Portland.

"Kurt's driving the equipment," Billy related. "In a van."

"And we'll be driving the tour bus," Pres added. Earlier that summer the band had purchased a small bus from an old rock band that had fallen on hard times.

"Where are we staying?" Emma asked, and everyone grinned. She was so caught up in the planning that for the moment she'd forgotten she couldn't go.

"We're going cheap," Pres said. "Bargain

motels all the way. Separate rooms for guys and girls."

"Drag!" everyone yelled at once.

"Even you and Carrie?" Sam joked.

"Yup," Billy said with a smile. "Low-rent tour. High-rent results. Any questions?"

Nobody had any.

"I've got one more piece of news," Billy said, scratching his chin. He looked over at Pres, then back at the group. "It's about Sly."

A hush seemed to fall over the room, even though nobody else had been talking. Sly Smith was the Flirts's original drummer. He'd left the band and been replaced by Jake Fisher because he'd developed full-blown AIDS earlier in the summer, and had to go back home to Maryland for hospital treatment. In his last letter, he'd told the band that his health was going downhill, and that he was losing his eyesight—maybe temporarily, maybe permanently, the doctors weren't sure. He'd told them that the best thing they could do for him was to be the best damn band in the world.

"I feel like a little kid," Billy said, shaking his head.

"Go on, man," Pres urged him, a twinkle in his eyes.

"I hate to jinx it by talking about it," Billy said to his buddy.

"Look," Pres said, "if you don't, I will." He smiled encouragingly at Billy.

"Okay," Billy said. He took a deep breath. "There's a chance Sly might come up for the tour."

"You're kidding," Sam said automatically.

"Nope," Pres assured her.

"It's true," Billy said, peeling at the label on his bottle with his right thumb. "Sly called us this afternoon. His doctors said if he's up to it, he could come along."

"How did he sound?" Sam asked warily.

"Beat," Billy answered honestly. "Whipped."

"Do you think he'll actually come?" Emma asked.

"You know Sly," Pres drawled. "And you know what this band meant to him. If there's a way, he'll be here."

"He'd hijack a plane if he needed to," Jay quipped.

"Could he play?" Emma asked shyly. "I mean, Jake, of course, is the—"

But the drummer interrupted her. "Man, from what I've heard, he's one hell of a rock and roll drummer. If he wanted to get behind the kit, I'd be honored."

Billy shook his head. "He's too weak," he said. "Way too weak."

"Reading between the lines, I'd say . . . well, I'd say this could be the last time we see him," Pres said quietly.

Everyone was silent for a moment.

"So there's a really special reason for this tour," Billy finally said. "Keep that in mind."

Emma looked at Sam, and Sam returned her pleading look.

I've got to find a way to go on this tour now, Emma thought. *There just has to be a way! Or I may never get to see Sly again.*

THREE

"Hey, Carrie, we're home," Graham Perry Templeton called out as he and his wife, Claudia, let themselves in through the front door of their palatial summer home.

"Hi! I'm in the family room," Carrie called back. She was sprawled out on one of the comfortable couches in the family room. Emma was next to her, sitting in one of the new oversized royal blue leather chairs Claudia had had shipped from New York.

It was later that night. Emma had called Carrie from the Flirts' house to see if she could stop over after the band practice.

"You're the smartest person I know,"

Emma had told her. “Maybe you can think of a solution to my unsolvable problem.”

Carrie, who had been stuck at the Templetons’ baby-sitting for Ian and Chloe, had urged Emma to stop by. “Although I don’t know if I can offer any brilliant suggestions,” she had added. “Maybe if we think about it together, though . . .”

“I hope so,” Emma had replied.

And so Emma had driven over. When she arrived, she had told Carrie all about Sly and his phone call to Billy and Pres that afternoon.

“So I’ve just got to figure out a way to go on this tour,” Emma had told Carrie. “Especially if Sly might be going.”

They had spent the next hour brainstorming, but hadn’t come up with any viable solutions by the time Claudia and Graham arrived home.

“Everything all right?” Claudia asked as she and Graham walked into the family room. They had been out to dinner at Les Marais, a very upscale French restaurant in Portland. “Oh, hi, Emma,” she added when she realized Carrie’s friend was there.

"Everything's fine," Carrie assured her employer. "The kids are in bed. Did you guys have fun?"

"I don't want to look at another French pastry as long as I live," Graham groaned, patting his stomach. "I don't care how good it looks."

"Wise idea," Claudia teased him. She reached over and gave Graham a playful squeeze.

"Is that any way to treat a superstar?" he asked, pretending to be hurt.

"Just so you don't turn into a superstar with a spare tire around your middle," Claudia said with a grin.

"One pastry doesn't hurt," Graham retorted, plopping into the chair opposite Emma.

"Until you get on the scale," his wife commented.

"Look, if I want you to nag me about my weight, I promise I'll let you know," Graham told Claudia, an edge to his voice.

"I take it that's my cue to back off," Claudia said evenly.

"You take it right," Graham said. "Anyway, no one recognized us. Or if they did, they had the good sense to let us eat in peace. That was fun."

Carrie nodded sympathetically. She knew it was hard for Graham, one of the world's biggest rock stars, to go out to dinner with his wife, when basically the whole world knew his face.

"Like your shirt," Graham said, grinning at Carrie.

Carrie looked down at her multicolored tie-dyed shirt. "Your kid's responsible—Chloe made it," she explained. "Tie-dyeing was our entertainment project yesterday."

"You're so good with her," Claudia said, her voice full of warm admiration.

"She's a great little girl," Carrie replied. "She really is."

"When she's not being a great little monster," Graham said with a laugh. He reached for the dish of chocolate kisses in the center of the coffee table.

"Graham!" Claudia admonished him. "We just ate dinner!"

"Look," he told his wife as he unwrapped the candy. "I am your husband. Your children are upstairs asleep. You get to tell them what to do. Not me." He popped the candy daintily into his mouth and reached for another.

Emma sneaked a surreptitious look at Graham's waistline to see if he looked fatter. *He looks great to me,* she thought. *I don't know what Claudia is complaining about!*

"I just don't want anything to happen to you," Claudia said, pushing her blond hair off her face.

Graham smiled at his wife, who was much younger than he was. "Oh, so that's the deal. This is about Allen Baker, right?"

"He was only two years older than you are right now," Claudia pointed out, her face suddenly looking distracted and cloudy.

"Allen Baker was my old keyboard player," Graham explained to Carrie and Emma. "He died of a heart attack a few days ago."

"That's terrible!" Carrie cried.

"Yeah, tell me about it," Graham agreed. He turned back to his wife. "But honey, Allen abused his body for years."

"So did you," Claudia reminded her husband.

Emma recalled that Graham had had a problem with cocaine in the past, but as far as she knew he hadn't touched drugs in a long time.

Graham got up and went to his wife. He pulled her to her feet and hugged her. "I'm not gonna die, baby," he told her. "You can't get rid of me that easily." Then, with his arm still around Claudia, he turned back to the girls. "So, what's going on with the Flirts? You guys psyched for the tour?"

Carrie looked quickly at Emma, then back at Graham. "There's kind of a problem."

"You've got the time off, no problem," Claudia reassured Carrie.

Carrie shifted her position in her chair. "Actually," she said, "it's Emma who's got a problem with the tour."

"What's up?" Graham asked.

Carrie quickly sketched out for Graham and Claudia Emma's situation with the Hewitts.

"That's a drag," Claudia said. She looked

at Emma. "You don't think you can get Jane to change her mind? You tried?"

"How can I even ask her?" Emma queried. "All she's doing is asking me to do my job!"

"No one can think of anything to do," Carrie said sadly. "Emma's really stuck."

Graham got a funny look on his face. "Maybe not," he said slowly. "Maybe not."

Claudia looked at her husband. "I know that look, Graham," she said, her voice mock accusing. "What are you thinking?"

"I'm thinking I'd like to help Billy and the band out, that's what I'm thinking," Graham said, pulling his wife closer.

Graham's tried to help the band before, Carrie recalled. *Back when Diana's father bought Polimar Records and Diana tried to take over the Flirts, Graham said that he'd get a demo tape of the Flirts to his own record company. But nothing ever really came of it. Billy was so disappointed. . . .*

"What do you think you can really do, Graham?" Claudia asked.

Graham raised his eyebrows. "I've

thought of something," he said slowly. "You might laugh, but it just might work."

"Graham Perry Templeton," Claudia said, "if this is one of your schemes . . ."

"What is it?" Emma asked, her eyes wide with hope.

"Here's the deal," Graham began.

"You're telling me that Ian's dad, Graham Perry, is coming over *to our house,* and I'm not gonna be here to see him?" Ethan Hewitt protested to his mother.

"That's right," Jane said as she handed Ethan his camp bag. "You're going to camp. Right now."

It was the next morning, and Graham Perry had just interrupted the Hewitt family's morning routine by telephoning Jane and asking if he could come over for a few minutes. Jane had never actually met Graham, but she did know that Ian and Ethan were friends, so she very readily agreed.

Please, please, let this work, Emma prayed. *It has to work!*

"That stinks," Ethan stated. "I've hardly

ever seen him when I've been over at their house. Sure I can't stay home from camp?"

"I'm sure," Jane said kindly. "Emma will be coming over to the club later with Katie and Wills."

Emma, who was standing in the doorway holding Katie's hand, nodded in agreement. "I'll be there soon."

"Okay, but I feel sick," Ethan said dramatically, grabbing at his throat as if he were choking. "I have a fever."

"There's nothing wrong with you," Jane said. "Here's your ride. Off you go!"

Ethan trudged out to the driveway where his ride was waiting.

I'm surprised Ethan hasn't met Graham, Emma thought. *He and Ian see each other fairly often. Maybe I'll ask Graham to autograph something that's in Ethan's room. Ethan probably felt funny asking Ian to get his dad's autograph. He was probably afraid it wouldn't be cool.*

Moments after the camp bus pulled out, Emma saw Graham's Mercedes pull into the driveway. Graham hopped out and bounded up the front walkway to the door. He was dressed casually in a pair of jeans and a T-shirt with Garth Brooks's picture on it.

Emma crossed her fingers for luck. *If Graham can pull this off,* she thought, *I will be in his debt forever.*

Jane opened the door and smiled warmly. "Hi!" she said. "I'm Jane Hewitt. It's a pleasure."

"Pleasure's mine," Graham said politely, holding out his hand. "My kid thinks the world of your kid. How're you doing, Emma?"

"Fine," Emma said casually, even though her heart was going a thousand beats per minute.

"Come in," Jane invited. "Can I get you some fresh coffee?"

"That'd be great," Graham said. "Do you think Emma can join us?"

"Sure, why not?" Jane said, her voice quizzical. She looked at Emma to see if she had any clue as to what was going on, but Emma quickly looked away.

Jane led the way into the kitchen, poured

Graham a cup of coffee from the Braun coffeemaker, and then joined Emma and Graham at the kitchen table.

"Listen, I just have to get this out of the way," Jane said, sipping her coffee. "My husband and I are huge fans of your music. In fact, we both fell in love with 'You're the One' when we were in college."

"You know, that means I'm old," Graham teased.

"Seasoned," Jane said with a grin. "Anyway, that's still my all-time favorite romantic ballad. And my husband, Jeff, is going to be devastated that he didn't get to meet you!"

After that the three of them exchanged pleasantries for a short time, and then Graham started to talk about why he'd come over.

"I understand Jeff's trying a case," he said.

"That's right," Jane said. "In Florida."

Graham looked at Emma. "Guess that means Emma's not going to be able to go on the Flirts' tour."

"That's right," Jane said. "I'm sorry, but I need her here. Work comes first."

"Of course," Graham agreed. "But what if she were to have a suitable replacement? Temporarily, of course. Just for those few days."

She's never going to go for it, Emma thought, sneaking a peek at Jane out of the corner of her eye.

"What do you mean?" Jane asked him. "I mean, not just anyone could replace Emma."

"Of course not," Graham agreed. "You'd need someone highly qualified."

"You have someone in mind?" Jane asked, a smile playing at the corners of her mouth. "You want to come take care of my kids?"

"I doubt I'm qualified," Graham said with a chuckle. "Just ask my own kids."

Jane laughed. "Well, it's a nice idea, Graham," she said. "But it's impossible, because—"

"What about Irene Wentworth?" Graham asked. "Have you heard of her?"

Jane's eyes widened. "Have I heard of her?" she echoed. "She's famous!"

Graham nodded. "She writes a column for *All-American Parenting* magazine."

"She was on one of the talk shows just the other day—I forget which one—and she was great," Jane said. She shook her head. "But you can't mean her, can you?"

Graham reached into his back pocket and pulled out a folded fax. He handed it to Jane. Emma watched as Jane read it, her face going from utter skepticism to total disbelief. Jane handed the fax to Emma when she was done, and Emma scanned it quickly.

I can't believe Graham pulled this off, Emma thought as she read. *Irene Wentworth says that she owes Graham a favor for allowing himself to be featured in her new book, and so she'll do it! She says she thinks it'd be great research for her column to actually live with a family like the Hewitts for a few days.*

It sure helps to be famous, Emma mused.

"Graham," Jane said, "I don't know how you did this on such short notice. I don't even want to know."

"So what's your answer?" Graham asked her.

"Yes, of course," Jane said. "So long as I can give a dinner party for her while she's here!"

"You'll have to ask her that yourself," Graham said, taking a sip of his coffee. Then he turned to Emma.

"Have fun on the tour," he suggested with a smile.

"Oh—oh—this is fantastic!" Emma cried. She jumped up and threw her arms around him, hugging him hard. Then she realized she was hugging a superstar, and she stepped away from him in embarrassment. "I'm sorry, I just—"

"Believe me, the hug was fine," Graham said. "And I'm really happy to help the Flirts out. I've always believed in Billy and Pres. I still do. They deserve a break. I'm glad I can give them a little one."

Emma turned to Jane. "I really, really appreciate this."

"I'm happy for you," Jane said sincerely. "And I'm happy for me, too!" She looked down at the fax with wonder.

"So, listen, it was really nice to meet you, Jane," Graham began as he got up from his chair.

Then Emma thought of one more thing.

I'm glad I remembered, she thought quickly.

"Graham?"

"Yeah?" Graham answered.

"Do you think you could come upstairs with me to Ethan's room?" Emma asked. "I've got a favor to ask you. I promise it'll take only a second. By the way, can you bring a pen?"

"Good-bye, Sunset Island!" Sam chortled. "Hello, big time!"

"Down, girl," Carrie cautioned.

"It's best not to get your hopes up too high," Emma reasoned. "The tour might not be a success."

"You know it will be a success, because we rule!" Sam cried.

The girls were sitting together on the boardwalk above the main beach. It was about five-thirty that same afternoon, and all three of them had come down to the beach for a couple of hours before they had to go to their respective employers' homes and prepare dinner for their families.

Emma had just told them what Graham had pulled off. She had already called Billy, who was really happy and relieved. He promised to pass the word to the rest of the guys.

"Tell me Graham isn't the coolest," Sam said. "If he were just a few years younger, I would have to jump his bones."

"Sam, he's married!" Emma said.

"Don't bother me with details," Sam said, waving her hand in the air. "Hey, we need to tell Erin, so we can decide which outfits we want to wear!"

"Oh, Sammi!" an all-too-familiar voice trilled from behind them. "And little washed-out Emma and chunky Carrie!" the voice added. "Aren't you just thrilled to run into them, Diana?"

"Positively ecstatic," another female voice agreed.

"I am so not up for this," Sam told her friends, grimacing slightly.

Emma sighed. Why did it seem that just

when things were going well, Lorell Courtland and Diana De Witt, the girls' archenemies, always showed up to put a damper on things?

"Well, if it isn't the last three virgins on Sunset Island," Diana marveled.

"Oh, I don't think so, Diana," Lorell told her friend dramatically. "I heard the chunky one will do it with anything that has a zipper!"

"She must mean you, Diana," Sam said nastily.

Lorell was from Georgia and had a soft Southern accent that she made sickeningly sweet whenever she was around Sam, Emma, and Carrie, mostly to cover up the really mean things she said.

And Diana, who'd gone to boarding school with Emma in Switzerland and knew her well, didn't even make an effort to cover up her nasty remarks. She seemed to take actual pride in them.

"I'm very choosy," Diana said coolly, tossing her head so that her perfect chestnut curls swayed. She smiled maliciously at

Emma. "For example, I chose Kurt. And I got Kurt. Kind of like that."

"He's back with Emma," Carrie said.

"Yes, I heard," Diana replied. "But only because I kicked him to the curb, so to speak."

"That's not true and you know it," Sam snapped. "He asked Emma to marry him, not you."

"Yes, we all know about that, too," Diana said in a bored voice. "Very old news, wouldn't you say?" she asked Lorell.

"Very," Lorell agreed.

"I've kind of been thinking more along the lines of, oh, Pres lately," Diana said casually. "He is looking awfully buff these days."

Sam took in Diana's perfect figure and gorgeous face. "He has zero interest in you," she told her.

"You wish," Diana said.

"He loves Sam," Emma said.

"Please," Diana scoffed. "He is not about to settle for greasy old Kansas hamburger anymore once I offer him steak!"

"You bitch—" Sam began.

Carrie reached for Sam's arm. "Come on," she said in a low voice. "She's only doing this to tick you off. She was always hitting on Pres when she was in the band, remember? And he totally rejected her!"

"I think my friend here was the one who did the rejecting," Lorell objected heatedly.

Carrie shook her head. "This is a stupid and juvenile conversation."

"You're so right," Diana agreed. "There's just something about the three of you that brings out the worst in me!"

She leaned against the low wooden railing separating the boardwalk from the beach's white sand. Lorell joined her.

Okay, Sam admitted to herself. *They look great. They're probably both better looking than me. And they've definitely got a lot more money than me. Not to mention hooters, an area where I am sadly deficient. Well, so what? Lorell and Diana are still the most obnoxious and pathetic people I've ever met.*

"So," Diana said, her gaze darting from Sam to Emma to Carrie and then back again, "I understand the Flirts are going on tour." She poked Lorell in the ribs, as if it were the funniest thing she'd ever heard.

"Can you believe it?" Lorell murmured.

"With No-Hooters on one side of the Poor Little Princess and the Cow on the other!" Diana laughed loudly.

Sam's ears burned. She knew that "No-Hooters" referred to her, and "the Cow" was a nasty crack about Erin Kane's weight. And the "Poor Little Princess" was obviously intended for Emma's benefit.

"Good thing we don't have you two," Sam cracked. "They'd have to pass out gas masks."

"Ooh!" Lorell cooed. "Was that a joke?"

"I don't know," Diana commented. "We'll have to check with Sam's interpreter."

"Why don't the two of you just leave?" Carrie suggested directly. "I mean, don't you get tired of this stupid game?"

"Yeah," Sam agreed. "In other words, don't you have a life?"

Diana looked at Emma shrewdly. "You're very quiet," she accused.

Emma shrugged. "Talking to you seems like a waste of energy."

Diana put her hands over her heart. "I'm just so wounded."

"She's deeply hurt," Lorell agreed.

"So," Diana said, straightening up, "did I mention that I'm thinking about starting my own band? My father plans to back it. With plenty of money. I'll be sure to send you a copy of our first demo."

"Don't bother," Sam said.

"Oh, but I insist," Diana said. "After all, when I beat you to a deal with Polimar, I think you deserve to know why!"

"Toodles!" Lorell called as she and Diana turned to leave. After a couple of steps, though, Diana turned back around. "Oh!" she said, as if she had the most important thing in the world to tell the girls. "I forgot to tell you something."

"I can't imagine you having something to say," Sam said acidly.

"But this," Diana corrected, "you will not want to miss." She smiled evilly. "Lorell and I have a little surprise for you guys in Bangor. A really nice little surprise."

"A great little surprise," Lorell said, fluttering her eyelashes.

"What is it?" Sam asked, and then hit herself in the head, mad at herself for giving the two of them such a setup line.

"You'll just have to wait," Diana said conspiratorially. "Bye!"

"Can you believe they actually think they have talent?" Lorell remarked casually to Diana. "Bye, y'all. See you soon!"

When Diana and Lorell had walked away, Emma turned to Carrie. "You know it's going to be something horrible."

"I know," Carrie agreed.

"Their idea of a nice surprise is a hit squad waiting for us," Sam groused. "She couldn't really put a band together fast enough to try to get our record deal at Polimar . . . could she?"

"No," Carrie said definitively. "Anyway, we'd probably know about it."

"How?" Sam demanded. "Tell me how."

"Billy," Carrie improvised. "He'd probably find out about it in advance."

"No, he wouldn't," Sam snapped. "Polimar wouldn't let him. Why would they? You know, I don't think anyone would put me in prison for killing her."

"You've said that before," Carrie reminded Sam.

"That doesn't make it less true," Sam said self-righteously.

Emma got a sinking feeling in her stomach. "Do you think it's true?" she asked in a small voice.

"Impossible," Carrie said firmly. "Anyway, it's not like there's only one recording contract to be had. She's just trying to scare us."

"That's right," Emma said. "That's all she's trying to do."

And succeeding, she added to herself as she suddenly shivered in the warm, late afternoon air. *Succeeding just fine.*

FOUR

"On the road again!" Sam sang as the Flirts' tour bus passed a sign on Interstate 95 that read BANGOR 6 MILES.

Billy looked back from the driver's seat. "You don't sound anything like Willie Nelson."

"Ha!" Sam said. "People only think he wrote that song. Actually, I wrote it, and I've been kind enough to give him credit."

"What a woman!" Pres marveled, pulling Sam to him in a hug.

Sam stuck out her lower lip, imitating a little kid, and her voice turned whiny. "Are we there yet, Dad? How much longer? I'm bored! I have to go to the bathroom!"

Everyone in the bus—Emma, Carrie,

Erin, Sam, Billy, Pres, Jay, and Jake—cracked up.

"Sam thinks she's four years old," Jake suggested, shifting his position against one of the bus windows.

"She's definitely regressing," Jay observed.

"I *am* four," Sam said with dignity. "I've been studying Chloe Templeton in my spare time."

It was four days later, and finally the big tour was starting. The last few days had been a whirlwind of activity. Every day there seemed to be band practice, more band practice, and more band practice. Sam had put together some new stage outfits for the girls. She had found some sheer black chiffon, which she had fashioned into simple, short, loose-fitting shifts held together with dozens of tiny rhinestone pins. Underneath the see-through shifts the girls wore antique slips with strategically placed rips in them. On their feet they wore black combat boots they had found cheap at an army-navy store. The outfits managed to flatter all three women, even though they were totally different physical types.

And to think I almost missed this, Emma thought. *Thank goodness for Graham. He really came through for me. Correction. For everyone.*

She stared out the window and watched the world go by. *I wish Kurt were on the bus with me,* she thought.

Kurt had left Sunset Island really early that morning in a van that carried all the band's equipment. He would be setting up at the Roadhouse, a hot new rock and blues club that had opened on South Orono Road in Bangor the summer before, and would have it ready by the time the band arrived. This was progress from their last tour, when they'd stuffed everything into the bus.

The band itself had left the island late in the morning, figuring on a three-hour drive up to Bangor, including a couple of pit stops.

Emma smiled at her friends. *I am so happy,* she thought. *What could be better than being on a rock tour with the people I love most in the world?*

She looked down at her satin baseball jacket and smiled again. Everyone in the bus was wearing the same jacket—with FLIRTING WITH DANGER printed on the back. *This group feels more like family than my real family,* she realized, a lump forming in her throat. *I don't think I can stand to see this summer end. . . .*

"You look thoughtful," Carrie said, cocking her head at Emma.

"I was just thinking about how happy I am," Emma said shyly.

"Me, too," Carrie said. She glanced up at Billy, who had his eyes on the road. "I'm happier than I've ever been in my life."

Emma thought about Carrie's recent crisis, when Billy had almost left the island for good to go help his family in Seattle. His dad was recovering from a serious accident, and his mother needed him.

I'm so glad Billy didn't stay in Seattle, Emma thought. *It would have been so awful.* She glanced at her watch. *Two-thirty. Right on time. So far, so good. But what about this surprise that Diana was talking about? I can't believe there's really anything that she could do, but you can never count Diana out!*

"Do you think we need to worry about Diana?" she asked Carrie.

"I heard that!" Sam called. "She was full of hot air. She just wanted us to be worried!"

"Why, what happened?" Pres asked.

"Oh, she invented some B.S. about how she had a surprise for us on our tour," Sam said. "She's just never gotten over the fact that Erin replaced her."

"But thank God you did," Emma told Erin.

"Thanks," Erin said.

"I'm pretty glad, too," Jake told Erin, pulling her close.

"Are we there yet?" Sam whined. "How much longer, Dad?"

Everyone laughed at Sam yet again and Billy steered the bus off the interstate onto the exit that led to downtown Bangor. He and Pres had also rented a couple of cellular telephones for the four-day tour, so that they could stay in touch with Kurt. And Kurt had called them earlier to tell them he had already booked two rooms at the Motel 6 on Orono Road.

"Remember the drill," Billy advised the band as he followed the signs to Orono Road.

"We know," Sam repeated. "Chill out for two hours—"

"Sound check at four-thirty," Jay chimed in.

"Gig at ten o'clock," Jake said.

"Sleep here, drive to Waterville tomorrow," Pres put in.

"And do it all over again!" Sam chortled.

Everyone laughed.

Billy slowed down. The Motel 6 was just ahead. He pulled the bus into the parking lot, quickly spotting Kurt's bright red equipment van in one of the parking spaces.

Kurt came bounding out of the room to meet them.

What's wrong, Emma thought. *He looks upset!*

"Hey, man," Billy said as he turned the

ignition off and jumped down out of the bus. "What's wrong?"

"Don't you answer your phone?" Kurt said angrily.

"Of course—" Billy began, but Kurt cut him off.

"I've been trying to call you every five minutes!" Kurt exploded. "The phone's been off!"

All of the others got out of the bus and gathered around Kurt and Billy.

"Whoa," Pres cautioned Kurt, "calm down, bro. Calm down."

Kurt shook his head. "Okay," he said, "I'll calm down. *You* get upset!" And he impatiently thrust the copy of the *Bangor Daily News* that he'd been holding in his left hand into Billy's face.

Billy took it and scanned it. The band pressed close so that they could read it, too.

And there it was. In a little box, at the bottom of the page.

Oh my God, Emma thought. *It's an advertisement for the Flirts' gig at the Roadhouse. And there's a notice that reads "cancelled" running right through it!*

"I don't believe this," Billy said.

"How could this have happened?" Jay asked.

"Someone messed up big-time," Pres said.

"But Kurt brought our equipment to the club!" Jay said. "Right?"

Kurt nodded vigorously as Emma moved close to him and reached for his hand. "Damn right I did," he said.

"Then how can—" Billy began.

"The club doesn't know anything about this!" Kurt shouted. "They claim the gig's still on!"

"But it's their ad!" Sam cried.

"They claim they didn't run it!" Kurt said.

"Jerks," Erin said.

"Hold on," Billy said. "You said the club doesn't know anything about this?"

Kurt nodded. "I bought the newspaper about a half an hour ago. When I saw the ad, I called the Roadhouse right away."

"And?" Pres prompted him.

"The manager said that as far as he knows," Kurt said, "the show's still on."

"Great," Pres expostulated. "We'll be there, the rep from Polimar will be there . . ."

"And no one else will be there," Billy finished. "Man, we are so, so screwed."

Sam clapped her hand to her face. "How could this have happened?" she moaned.

And then it hit Emma. *Diana. Diana did it. This was her little surprise.*

"I think I know who did this," Emma said softly.

"Who?" everyone asked her at once.

Emma looked at Carrie, then at Sam. "Think about it," she said. There was a beat of silence.

"Diana!" Sam finally shouted. "Oh my God, this is what she was talking about on the boardwalk! I'm going to kill her, and you are all going to help me!"

"Let's get our stuff inside," Billy advised. "Then we'll figure out what to do."

"Diana De Bitch deserves to die," Sam groused.

"You've said that fifty times already," Carrie told her. "It doesn't help."

"I should have known," Emma sighed.

She took a sip of some bottled water she'd brought with her.

"How could you have known she'd do something like *this*?" Billy said, leaning back against the motel bed.

"Nothin' you could do," Pres agreed.

It was about fifteen minutes later. The whole band, and Kurt and Carrie, were packed into one of the motel rooms they had taken for the night.

"Maybe so, maybe not," Sam said.

"What could you have done?" Billy challenged her.

Sam drew her finger across her throat in one quick slicing motion. Then she dropped off the bed where she was sitting and rolled around on the floor, clutching her throat in mock agony.

"I'm convinced," Kurt said, nodding. "But I'd suggest a hacksaw."

"That doesn't help us much now," Pres commented.

"We gotta figure out something to save this gig," Billy agreed.

"Right," Sam said sourly. "Maybe we can put out our own newspaper."

Billy's eyes lit up. "That's good thinking, Sam," he said.

"What?"

"Gimme the phone," he commanded, reaching for the yellow pages that was in the nightstand just to the left of the bed. He quickly flipped to the listing for radio and television stations.

"What are you doing?" Kurt asked, but Billy ignored him as he ran his finger up and down the small listings.

"Bingo," Billy said.

"What—"

Billy waved Kurt off as he quickly dialed the number he'd found.

"Is this WHOT rock radio?" he asked.

Carrie and the rest of the gang found themselves listening to only Billy's side of the conversation, but from what Billy was saying they could very easily figure out what was going on.

"This is Billy Sampson from Flirting With Danger," Billy said. "We sent you a demo of 'Love Junkie' a couple of weeks ago." He listened for about thirty seconds.

"Of course it's me!" he exploded. "We're here to do the gig at the Roadhouse!"

The others looked on anxiously.

"It's not cancelled!" Billy exclaimed.

Sam began twisting the ends of her hair.

"The club did *not* call you!" Billy said desperately. "That was someone faking it!"

Pres shifted uneasily in his chair.

"I'm serious!" Billy remonstrated, his face getting all flushed.

This is unbelievable, Emma thought, watching Billy turning redder and redder. *How could Diana do something like this?*

"If you don't believe me," Billy said with an exasperated look on his face, "call the club!"

Silence.

"You want me to prove who I am?" Billy asked. "How can I do that? All I know is that I'm here in a motel room in Bangor, ready to go onstage tonight at ten o'clock!"

"Tell him to look on the demo," Pres hissed quickly. "Tell him the date on the demo."

Billy stuck his hand over the receiver. "What *is* the date?" he asked Pres.

Pres grinned a little, and reached into his back pocket. He pulled out an actual copy of the demo tape and handed it to his partner.

"Look," Billy said into the phone, glancing down at the tape, "the demo comes in a green cassette box." He listened. "You want more? Okay, here's more. The label on the tape is orange."

Silence. Sam thought she would scream.

"More? My name's second on it, after Presley Travis's. And the date on the label—"

There was a brief pause.

"You believe me now?" Billy asked. "Then you've got to help me!"

Quickly Billy sketched out his idea—for the radio station to announce on the air several times between now and the time of the gig that the ad in the paper had been in error, and that the Flirts were indeed playing at the Roadhouse that night.

"Thanks, man," Billy said when the conversation was coming to a close. "I don't know how we can ever repay you." He listened for a moment, and a grin appeared on his face. "I'll think about it," he said. "Okay, I've thought about it. I'll do it!"

Billy hung up the phone. "Thanks, Sam," he said. "That was a great idea."

"But—" Sam began.

"It's a start," Billy said. "But there's a lot more we can do. We just have to think of it."

"I've got a few ideas," Emma said tentatively.

"Cool," Billy said. "Let's hear them."

"Hey, Red!" someone yelled from a passing car. "Want some help?"

Sam made a face as the car sped by.

"I'll pass," she said to Carrie, who was standing next to her.

"Good idea," Carrie suggested.

"He wasn't cute enough," Sam noted, flopping down on the grass and looking at her watch.

It was five-thirty that same afternoon. Sam should have been at the Roadhouse, going through the band's sound check, but Pres and Billy had decided that they were going to do the sound check solo, and that everyone else should spend the rest of the afternoon trying to build an audience for the night's performance.

Sam, Carrie, and Emma had spent the last hour and a half posting makeshift flyers about that night's show. It was a hot day, and Sam was whipped.

"I'm exhausted," Sam said, wiping her brow with a red bandanna she took out of the pocket of her cutoff shorts.

"Only two hundred more to go," Carrie noted wryly, looking down at the box of flyers that the band had quickly put together at a copy shop near their motel. They were not elegant, but they were certainly serviceable enough.

The Flirting With Danger show
isn't cancelled!
10:00 tonight, at
the Roadhouse. Party on!
C U there!

And then she looked back down the street that they had been walking along.

Tacked to every telephone pole, on both sides of the street, was one of the flyers.

"What if no one comes?" Sam moaned.

"They'll come," Carrie assured her. "If we get these posted."

I hope they'll come, Emma said to herself. *Because if it were me, and I got one story from the newspaper ad, another from a radio station, and I saw these flyers up on telephone poles, I'd probably just stay home, right?*

"This is a nightmare," Sam said flatly.

"I know," Carrie agreed, sitting down next to her friend. Emma remained standing.

"And the Polimar rep is supposed to be there!" Sam cried. "What if there aren't any people?"

"There'll be people," Carrie assured her.

"But what if there aren't?" Sam repeated.

Carrie shrugged.

"Diana De Witt, I hate your guts!" Sam screamed at the top of her lungs. Then she turned to Carrie. "There, I feel better now."

Carrie nodded. "Me, too." She smiled.

But what if no one comes? Emma thought anxiously. *What if Sam's right? Then this tour is going to be over before it even gets started.*

FIVE

"We're screwed," Sam said with fake cheerfulness as she wandered back into the Flirts' tiny, overheated dressing room behind the stage at the Roadhouse. It was at least ninety degrees in the dressing room, but the mood of the band hardly matched the temperature.

Emma's heart sank down into the pit of her stomach. It was clear that the Flirts were in trouble. Big trouble.

Sam had just been out front in the Roadhouse, a big, cavernous club that was in a converted furniture warehouse. Billy had sent her on a mission: to check out what kind of a crowd the Flirts had drawn for their gig after their afternoon of emergency crowd-building measures. Everyone had been hopeful that the work would pay off.

Kurt would have been out front, doing the checking, but he was still somewhere on the streets of Bangor, trying to get people to come to the show.

The band was scheduled to go onstage at ten that night, and it was already ten minutes past ten. The Flirts were stalling as best they could.

From what Sam is saying, the news can't be too good, Emma thought.

"How bad is it?" Billy asked. He was sitting on the one couch in the dressing room, next to Pres. Each of them held a cold bottle of fruit juice in his hands, and they were dressed in their usual stage clothes—jeans, and T-shirts of classic bands. Billy's T-shirt was emblazoned with a photo of The Who, while Pres had an old Jackson Browne shirt.

Sam leaned against the pillar in the middle of the room. "How bad is it?" she echoed, her voice still cheerful. "It's terrible. Worse than terrible. It sucks. That's how bad."

"Then what do you sound so happy about?" Jay asked, his voice uncharacteristically testy.

"It's better than throwing things," Sam replied with a shrug.

"How bad exactly, Sam?" Erin asked as she refastened a tiny heart-shaped rhinestone pin on her right side.

"Well," Sam said, "the good news is that there will be more people out there in the audience than there'll be on stage."

"And the bad news?" Pres asked, pulling himself to his feet.

"Not many more," Sam said flatly.

"Damn," Billy said under his breath. "Damn, damn, damn."

"Chill, pardner," Pres said to him softly. "That guy from Polimar never made it here."

"That's right," Jake said, running a drumstick through his swept-back black locks. "We've dodged a big bullet."

Billy shook his head. "It's a bad omen, man," he said. "I don't like it."

"That radio station thing didn't help much, huh?" Pres asked.

"They asked me to thank them from the stage, in return for making an announcement on the air," Billy said. "Thank them for what?"

"It was a good try," Carrie said encouragingly. Billy gave her a helpless look. She reached for his hand and held it tightly.

One of the managers from the club—a slight woman with boyishly short hair—stuck her head in the dressing room.

"You guys ready?" she asked.

"For what?" Jay asked morosely.

"We're ready," Billy said, tossing Jay a look.

"Then let's get going," she urged. Without waiting for Billy's reply, she closed the door.

"Like she cares," Jay said sourly. "Gimme a break."

"She gets her guarantee," Jake agreed, his voice downcast.

Billy got to his feet. "Okay," he commanded sharply. "Enough of that."

"What, are you gonna tell us to have a

good attitude?" Jay asked. "I played for more people than this with my garage band when I was fourteen!"

"The Zits get bigger crowds," Sam said, referring to Ian Templeton's industrial-rock band, Lord Whitehead and the Zit People.

"Hey, we're professionals," Billy said sharply. "We're gonna act like it, no matter what."

Billy's right, Emma thought. *This is not the best way to start a show—with a bad attitude.*

"We're gonna play," Billy continued, "and we're gonna play hard. Everyone got that?"

Everyone nodded except Jay, and he finally nodded, too.

"Those people out there deserve our best," Pres said, "so let's give it to them."

"Rah, rah, rah, yeaaaaah team!" Sam shouted, as if she were a cheerleader back in high school.

Everyone looked at her.

"Sorry," Sam said, her voice small. "Just getting fired up."

"Let's go," Billy ordered. And he led the

band out onto the Roadhouse's oversized stage.

As soon as the band came onto the stage from the left-hand side, a bank of spotlights flashed, red and blue lasers danced crazily, and the sound of a bass drum—recorded, because Jake hadn't even gotten behind his drum kit yet—filled the air.

Emma got that familiar rush of excitement—the one she hadn't ever known before she joined the band, but which she now recognized from every single time she'd been onstage with them.

But something's wrong, Emma realized as she took her place at the backup singers' mike, blinded temporarily by the spotlights. *There's something completely wrong here.*

And then she realized what it was.

It's silent out there, she thought. *Usually everyone's yelling and screaming. But I don't hear a single voice from the crowd!*

"Hello, Bangor!" Billy yelled, out of habit.

"Hello, Flirts!" a couple of forlorn voices yelled back. They sounded weak in the cavernous rock and roll club.

Billy turned to the band and shrugged. He gave the hand signal that started them on their signature song, "Love Junkie."

You want too much
And you want it too fast
You don't know nothin'
About making love last.
You're a love tornado
That's how you get your kicks
You use me up
And move on to your next fix. . . .
You're just a Love Junkie
A Love Junkie, baby
A Love Junkie
You're driving me crazy. . . .

At the end of the first verse, Emma and the girls sang, "Love, love junkie, baby!" three times into their mikes. Then they did a spin move—Emma, who was in the center, to the left, and Sam and Erin to the right, which brought them back to face the audience.

"Oooooh!" the three of them sang together, for all they were worth.

Billy picked up the vocals for the second verse of the song and sang it with even more energy than usual. And then he tore through the final electric guitar riff as if he were ripping a sheet of newspaper in half.

Wow, Emma thought, *that's the best I've ever heard him play.* Out of the corner of her eye she could see that Sam and Erin were both shaking their heads slightly in appreciation of Billy's brilliance.

But the end of the song was an anticlimax. The last note sort of hung in the air, echoing around the walls of the steel-framed building. The two dozen or so people in the club applauded enthusiastically, but the applause sounded as feeble in the huge performance space as the earlier yells and calls had.

"I love Diana," Sam mumbled under her breath. "I want to have her love child."

"I love her more," Erin mumbled back.

A lump rose in Emma's throat. If things didn't get better soon, this night was going to be a total washout. But it didn't look as though things were going to get better anytime soon.

Billy led the band through three more of their songs: "You Take My Breath Away," "Wild Child," and "Ride the Wave."

Each time, Billy led the song as if the Roadhouse were packed to the rafters with people. And each time the reaction of the crowd got a little quieter.

"We should give it up," Sam grumbled at the end of "Ride the Wave."

"We can't quit," Erin said. "How would that look?"

"Better than standing out here," Sam commented. "This sucks."

The audience isn't applauding harder because there are hardly any of them out there! Emma thought.

At the end of "Ride the Wave," Billy turned to Pres, who was standing next to him, and conferred with him a moment. Pres listened intensely, giving a quick series of nods.

What are they doing? Emma thought. *Are we quitting for the night?*

Emma and the other backups watched, dumbfounded, as Pres unslung his electric guitar and went to get his acoustic one. Billy did the same thing.

"What are they doing?" Sam asked.

"Beats me," Erin replied.

Emma shrugged, too. This was not in the band's game plan for the evening.

"We're gonna give you a little treat," Billy said into the mike in front of him.

"Yippee," a guy in the back yelled out with sarcasm.

"Shut up, man!" someone yelled at the first guy. Then he called up to the stage, "Keep on rockin', bros!"

"Thanks, man," Billy called back to the fan.

"We're gonna give you the Flirts, unplugged," Pres drawled.

"Cool, man!" the guy yelled out.

"Y'all gotta come down front, though," Pres told them, "or this ain't gonna work."

Emma knew what Billy and Pres were doing. She'd once watched an *MTV Unplugged* show with Katie Hewitt, who'd recently gotten into watching the music video channel. The show had featured the rock and roll star Eric Clapton, and Clapton, who usually played electric music, only used his acoustic guitar.

Pres's words worked like magic. Emma watched as the forty people in the club—she'd underestimated by a dozen or so, as some stragglers had come in late—wandered down to the front, and, just like she'd seen on MTV, sat on the floor.

Billy, meanwhile, had gone offstage and come back with a couple of stools. Nonchalantly he placed the stools at the front of the stage, and he and Pres climbed onto them with their acoustic instruments.

"So," he asked the crowd conversationally, not even using the mike, "what do you wanna hear?"

"'Layla'!" someone in the crowd joked, and Emma recognized the title as one of the songs that Clapton himself had sung on the MTV show.

"That's not a Flirts song," Sam hissed to Erin and Emma.

"'Layla'?" Pres asked, his voice mellow and relaxed. "You want 'Layla'?"

"Yeah!" the same person said. A couple of others cheered, too.

"Cool. You got it," Billy replied. And he quickly launched into the famous guitar riff that starts the classic rock tune.

Emma and the other backup singers watched him and Pres, totally amazed.

Emma was awakened by the sound of pounding at the front door of the motel room she was sharing with Sam, Erin, and Carrie.

"Who's there?" Sam called out sleepily. She and the other girls had been awakened, too.

It was the morning after the disastrous gig at the Roadhouse—a gig that Emma felt had been only somewhat salvaged by Pres and Billy's quick decision to turn the evening into a night of the Flirts unplugged.

And because the Polimar rep never arrived, Emma recalled. *Thank goodness for that. What if he had been there?*

"It's me!" a familiar voice called. "It's Kurt! Open up! Quick!"

"Hold on!" Sam yelled back. "Lemme put on some clothes."

"Hurry up!" Kurt cried.

"Stay in bed," Erin commanded her friends. "I'm closest to the door—I'll get it."

She hopped out of bed, wrapped a big robe around herself, and opened the door. The other girls just pulled the covers up over themselves—Emma and Sam were sharing one huge double bed, and Carrie was in the other one.

Kurt came bounding into the room, grinning happily. He ran over to Emma and gave her a big kiss.

"We did it!" he cried, his voice full of joy.

"I haven't even brushed my teeth!" she yelped. "How can you kiss me?"

"Who cares?" Kurt cried. "Look at this!" He tossed that day's *Bangor Daily News* to Carrie, and stuck another copy in Emma and Sam's faces.

"What is it?" Emma asked.

"Read!" Kurt ordered, and pointed to an article on the entertainment page.

FLIRTS STUNNING IN UNPLUGGED DEBUT

by Harpeth Hall

The expected huge crowd at the Roadhouse never materialized last night, due to some confusion about whether or not the gig by Flirting With Danger, a group from Sunset Island, was cancelled.

It wasn't. And the forty or so brave souls who ventured out to hear Maine's best band were amply rewarded for their efforts.

The Flirts' electric set was just plain hot. And the decision by Billy Sampson, the Flirts' lead singer, to turn the second half of the show into an extended unplugged set was nearly as inspired as the music that ensued.

A lesser band might have thrown in the towel when it looked out from the stage and saw the dismally small crowd gathered to hear them. Not the Flirts, however. If anything, it seemed as if the small crowd charged Billy Sampson and his band with electricity.

And lightning struck. Boy, how it struck.

Emma read on eagerly. The reporter went on and on about the show—he'd obviously been one of the few people in the audience, and no one in the band had had any clue that he was there.

"Thank you, God!" Sam exclaimed when she saw where the article was heading.

"No," Carrie said. "Thank you, Billy."

"Both!" Sam decided happily.

Emma couldn't agree more.

SIX

"I can't believe they're both on the same flight," Sam exclaimed as she pressed her nose against the glass in the small waiting area at Waterville Airport. The early afternoon sun shone in brightly.

"Believe it," Carrie said to her as she waited alongside her friend.

"Makes my life easy," Kurt, who was standing to Carrie's left, cracked. "I don't have to play taxi driver twice."

"C'mon, you're used to it," Sam joked.

Everyone laughed, knowing that Kurt had a job back on Sunset Island as a taxi driver.

I hope they both actually show up, Carrie

thought. *Though I don't know how I'll react to Sly. . . .*

It was the same day, about three hours after Kurt had burst into the girls' motel room with the good news about the article.

The band had packed up quickly in Bangor, stowing their gear in the van Kurt was driving and piling into the bus. They'd driven in a convoy south on Interstate 95 toward Waterville, about sixty miles away.

They'd dropped Erin and Jake off at the Holiday Inn on Elm Street—she'd pleaded exhaustion, but Carrie suspected that the two of them might be just taking a little private time for some romance—and then drove to the airport.

Kurt had gotten two phone calls early in the morning in Bangor, saying that both Shelly Plotkin, the record-label executive, and Sly Smith were arriving on the two o'clock commuter flight from Portland.

"I hope Plotkin actually shows up," Billy said anxiously.

"He will," Carrie told him warmly.

"I hope so. . . ." Billy's voice trailed off.

Everyone knew what he was thinking.

While it wasn't such a bad thing that Shelly hadn't made it to the gig at the Roadhouse the night before, the Flirts now had only three shows with which to impress the guy who'd be making the decision about their recording contract.

"Oh, he'll be here, all right," Jay, who was sitting on one of the cheap folding chairs nearby, reading the Waterville *Morning Sentinel,* commented. "Or I'll just kill him myself."

"They'd better get here soon," Sam said. "I'm hungry."

"You're always hungry," Pres joked, reaching in his pocket and tossing Sam a piece of taffy. She took it, unwrapped it, and popped it into her mouth.

"Anyone else want one?" Pres asked.

"I'm too nervous to eat," Emma said, making a face.

"Not *moi*!" Sam cried. "Hey, throw me more!" She was speaking around a wad of sticky taffy, and her voice sounded a little strange.

Billy looked at his watch. "It's due about now," he said.

"Here it comes," Carrie noted. A bright red propeller-driven airplane that looked as though it could carry about thirty people skimmed down and landed smoothly on the runway.

Emma looked over at Carrie, who nodded almost imperceptibly.

I guess she's nervous about this, too, Emma realized. *I admit it. I'm scared about seeing Sly. I've never seen anyone who's really sick with AIDS before. I'm really afraid I'll say something stupid.*

Billy ran his hand nervously through his hair. "Just remember, however Sly looks, he's still Sly."

Emma looked around at the group. They were all suddenly quiet and grim-faced, as though they were thinking deep thoughts. Even Sam had a serious look, and her usually wisecracking mouth was tight-lipped.

The plane rolled to a stop right in front of the waiting area, and a short staircase was wheeled out to meet it. The plane door swung out and open, and passengers started disembarking.

"That's Shelly!" Sam said loudly, as a small, somewhat bald man wearing jeans and a too-loud Hawaiian shirt came bounding down the stairs, first off the plane. He was directed to a mobile baggage cart.

Emma kept watching as other passengers got off. And then, finally, the flow of passengers stopped.

"Where's Sly?" Billy asked no one in particular. "Where is he?"

"Beats me," Pres replied. "He oughta be on that plane."

"Well, he ain't," Sam said flatly. "They just closed the door."

"Oh, hell," Billy said grimly. "I hope—"

"You don't think—" Pres said at the same time. They looked at each other.

"I don't know, man," Billy replied. "I just don't know. He was really sick."

I know what they're thinking, Emma thought, her face turning pale. *That the reason Sly isn't on that flight is that he suddenly got even sicker.*

And then Emma had a horrifying thought. *What if he's dead? What if Sly died this morning, while we were having such a great time on the ride down from Bangor?*

"Should we—" Emma began. She stopped, not wanting to say it.

"Let's go ask," Carrie said.

"I'll go with you," Emma said.

Her palms got sweaty as she and Carrie went over to one of the flight attendants, who had just walked into the small terminal.

"Excuse me," Emma said to the flight attendant.

"Yes?" he replied, stopping in his tracks.

"Our friend Sly Smith was supposed to be on that flight," Emma said, her voice catching in her throat.

"Smith?" the attendant asked. "Hold on."

He went over to a telephone that was on the wall and dialed a few numbers quickly. Emma grabbed Carrie's hand and held on tightly. She could feel herself go numb with fear.

I know he's dead, she thought. *I just know it.*

Then Emma overheard what the flight attendant was saying on the telephone.

"Smith missed the plane?" he said. "Thanks."

Emma shouted with happiness. "He's alive, he just missed the plane!" she told Carrie excitedly.

"Oh, I'm so glad!" Carrie cried, throwing her arms around Emma and hugging her hard. "You guys!" she called to the group as they ran back to their friends. "He's okay! He just missed the plane!"

"I'll kill him myself," Jay growled, in exactly the same tone that he'd used when he'd been referring to Shelly Plotkin just a few moments before.

And everyone cracked up—just as Sheldon Plotkin came through the door into the terminal. He was carrying a small suit bag over his shoulder.

"Well, well," he said with a grin, "a happy band! Far out! I love a happy band! You guys are beautiful!" He stuck his hand out for somebody to shake.

Billy reached for it. "Welcome to Waterville, Shelly," he said. Then the whole band gathered around, offering greetings to the Polimar Records exec.

Shelly grinned wildly. "That's it, Billy, call me Shelly!"

"You got it, Shelly," Billy agreed. "We're looking forward to having you see the show."

"You are?" Shelly asked. "Not as much as I am!" He laughed happily. "You know I've always believed in you guys. And that's from the heart, you know?"

"Then why doesn't he ever do anything for us?" Sam whispered to Emma, but Emma just nudged her in the ribs, indicating that Sam should shut up.

"So, how was your first gig?" Shelly asked eagerly as they walked toward the tour bus.

"Great," Billy said. "We got a really fantastic review in the local paper."

"Far out!" Shelly said. "I'm smelling success here, people!"

Emma saw Billy look at Carrie and roll his eyes, but he was smart enough to keep his mouth shut.

So I guess we'll all kiss up to him for the next few days, Emma said to herself. *Shelly might be a jerk, but he can do big things for us. And this just might be our very last shot.*

"You know what déjà vu is?" Emma asked as she, Sam, and Carrie sat together, side by side, on the steps of Colby College's library.

"Déjà vu?" Sam asked. "Is it a nudie bar in Portland?"

Carrie laughed. "Not exactly," she said. "It's like when you feel you're doing something you've already done or having a conversation you've already had, right?"

Emma nodded. "That's how I just felt. And then I realized I really *have* been here before!"

It was a few hours later. Emma, Sam, and Carrie were due for their sound check at Up Front, the rock and roll club on Front Street, at seven o'clock. Kurt was already at the club, setting up. So while Billy and Pres were in a business meeting with Shelly, and Erin, Jake, and Jay were back resting at the motel, the three girls had decided to take a walk around Colby College, the famous small liberal arts college that was up on a hill overlooking Waterville.

"There's nothing else to do," Sam had sniffed.

"You could go back and take care of the Jacobs kids," Carrie had observed.

"Which way's Colby?" Sam had answered quickly.

They'd bought some bottles of juice and split the cost of a taxi up to the campus. After spending an hour or so walking around it, checking out the gorgeous new theater and the art museum, they were resting together in front of the impressive library building.

"When were you here?" Carrie asked Emma.

"Remember that mix-up when Kurt was in jail?" Emma asked, taking a sip of her juice.

"Yup," Sam quipped. "Kurt the felon."

"Darcy, Molly, and I stopped here on the way up to Bangor," Emma recalled, a little wistfully. "When we were trying to prove that he had been framed." Sam swiveled her head to follow a good-looking guy who had just emerged from the library. She let out a loud whistle, and the guy turned around.

Sam waved to him.

"Down, girl," Carrie cautioned her.

"Hey, I'm just letting him know I appreciate good art," Sam cracked.

"Good art?" Emma asked.

"His body," Sam noted.

Fortunately, the guy apparently thought Sam was an acquaintance, so he only waved back instead of coming over to them.

"A lot has happened with me and Kurt," Emma said softly as she extended her legs.

"Have you talked to your mother lately?" Carrie asked.

Emma shook her head. "Not really."

"I still can't believe she cut you off!" Sam exclaimed.

"I can," Emma said ruefully.

"So, how does it feel to be poor like the rest of us?" Sam asked directly. "I mean, now that it's official."

"Sam," Carrie cautioned, "maybe you ought to just drop it."

"I'm only asking," Sam defended herself.

"We're best friends. Emma doesn't have to hide anything from us."

"You don't have to talk about it if you don't want to," Carrie said to Emma.

Emma took another sip of juice. "I don't mind," she answered.

"So," Sam commanded, "talk!"

"It's terrible," Emma said finally. "I hate it. I hate not having money. And I hate admitting that."

"I knew it," Sam yelped. "You're sorry you told your mother you wouldn't break up with Kurt."

"No," Emma answered, her tones measured. "I'm not sorry. Can you imagine if I had actually broken up with the guy I love—even temporarily—because my mother blackmailed me into it? She would think she could buy me forever. How could I live with that?" She sighed, shifting to a more comfortable position on the steps.

"I just hate not having money. It's kind of . . . depressing. It's just that . . . I grew up with it, and it was always there. Maybe it's the only thing I had in common with my parents," Emma struggled to explain. "And now, it's like *everything* has been cut off."

"I know, Em. It's depressing for us, too," Carrie offered.

Emma looked at her closely. "What do you mean?"

"Well," Carrie said, "I guess I can only speak for me, but I got used to your having money all the time."

"I never thought about that," Emma said.

"I feel kind of guilty admitting this," Carrie said. "But . . . well, it was really nice! I mean, you took us to California, you took Sam to Paradise Island; if either of us was short when we went out you always paid . . ."

"Those were the days," Sam said wistfully.

Emma shrugged. "I guess I'm not quite so wonderful a friend now that I'm broke."

"I didn't mean that!" Carrie insisted. "We love you, rich or poor!"

"Not me," Sam said. "I demand money!"

Emma gave her a hurt look.

"I'm kidding, girlfriend!" Sam said, grabbing Emma's arm. "You have to know I'm kidding! Anyway, it's not like we *always* let you pay."

"I know," Emma said quietly. *At least I think I know,* she added in her mind. She picked up a stray stone and cast it toward a tree.

"Maybe your mother will change her mind," Carrie told Emma.

"Maybe," Emma said, but she didn't feel very hopeful. "My father is planning to have a talk with her."

"You think she still loves him?" Sam asked.

"I don't know," Emma said thoughtfully. "I'm not sure my mother knows what love is."

"Me either," Sam said. Her friends looked at her. "What, you're so sure you know what love is?"

"I know I love Billy," Carrie said.

"And I know I love Kurt," Emma added.

"Yeah, but what does that mean?" Sam prodded. "Like, how often have girls thought they totally loved some guy, and then six months later they hated his guts?"

No one had a ready answer.

"So you see," Sam said smugly, "no one knows what love is."

"It's . . . it's caring about someone else more than you care about yourself," Carrie ventured.

"Sometimes I think love is just some big illusion," Emma said softly. Her friends looked at her. "What I mean is, sometimes I think we fall in love with the fantasy we make up about another person. We love who we want that person to be."

"This is getting way too out-there for me," Sam said, scratching a mosquito bite on her leg.

"Maybe it gets easier to figure out as you get older," Carrie said with a shrug.

"Yeah," Sam agreed. "Who cares about all that heavy stuff? We're young, we're foxes, we're in a cool band. What more is there?"

"I wonder what it's like to get old," Carrie mused.

"What's old?" Emma asked.

Carrie shrugged. "Fifty?"

"Fifty is ancient!" Sam exclaimed. "Thirty

sounds like the end of fun, if you ask me." She shuddered. "God, I hope I've married some really rich dude by that time."

"How about making your own money?" Carrie suggested.

"That's cool, too," Sam agreed. "I'm willing to spend mine, his, whatever!"

Carrie and Emma laughed along with Sam, but at the same time Emma felt thoughtful. And it was Sly who was on her mind.

He doesn't have the luxury of wondering what his life will be like ten years from now. How can he possibly deal with knowing that he's going to die?

And how will all of us live through it?

SEVEN

"What's the good word?" Billy asked Sam as she came back into the dressing room.

Sam grinned from ear to ear. "Packed," she pronounced. "Like sardines."

"All right," Pres drawled, his smile matching hers.

"I'm so glad!" Emma added.

"You people are beautiful!" Shelly Plotkin crowed. "This is magic night, guys!"

Just then Carrie, who'd been out front in the huge crowd that had gathered for the Flirts' gig, taking pictures of some of the club-goers, pushed her way into the dressing room. She was visibly sweaty.

"It's a madhouse out there," Carrie told

them, wiping the back of her arm across her forehead. "Anything to drink back here?"

Billy tossed her the plastic bottle of mineral water he'd been drinking.

"Pour it on your head," Sam suggested.

Carrie smiled, and instead put the bottle to her lips and took an enormous swallow.

It was nearly ten o'clock that evening, and the band—as well as Shelly Plotkin—was gathered together in the dressing room of Up Front, getting ready for the second night of their minitour.

There'd been no further problems with Diana De Witt. In fact, it seemed as though the club had done its publicity job as well as it possibly could. There wasn't an empty space in the house—it was wall-to-wall people, according to Sam's report.

The Flirts were set to go on at ten o'clock, and this time there'd be no stalling.

"Awesome, awesome, awesome," Shelly pronounced, mopping his sweaty brow with a red bandanna. "Let's rock and roll!"

Sam turned and looked at him. Shelly had changed shirts, and he was now wearing one that was, if anything, even louder and more gaudy than the one he'd had on before.

"You're Mr. Enthusiasm tonight, Shelly," she joked.

"Yessir!" Shelly chirped, practically rubbing his hands together with glee. "Hot night, hot music, hot babes—I mean, hot beat! That's what it's all about! That's why I'm in this business!"

Someone from the club stuck his head in. "Flirts, you're on!" he shouted.

Billy stood up and motioned for the band to draw near him. Sam moved in close to Pres, who took her hand in his and gave it a special squeeze.

Emma let her eyes rove over the group, and she felt a lump in her throat. *This really could be it,* she thought, and shivered. *This could be the start of something big.*

"Okay," Billy said quietly, his voice steely. "Let's go out there and blow this crowd away. We're not doing it for Shelly, either," he added. "We're doing it for Sly."

Everyone nodded. Although Sly still hadn't shown up, they had received word from a friend of his who had called that afternoon, telling them that Sly was still planning to come up.

The whole band left the dressing room and walked together to a small waiting area backstage.

The same guy who had poked his head into the dressing room before now walked out on the stage. A wall of noise from the crowd hit him full force. He grinned at the huge cheer.

"Are you ready to party?" the guy yelled out, his voice amplified by the live mike.

"*Yeeah!*" the crowd yelled back.

"I can't hear you!" the man replied.

"*Yeeeeaaah!*" the crowd screamed. Then someone threw a water balloon at the guy onstage. He instinctively reached for it, and it burst when it hit his hand.

The guy wiped his face with his wet hand, and the crowd went absolutely wild.

"This is intense," Erin Kane said to Emma and Sam, who were standing right near her.

"Unbelievable," Sam agreed.

"Pretty amazing," Emma added.

"All right!" the guy onstage shouted. "Let's give an H-2-O-ville greeting to the band you've been waiting for, Flirting With Danger!"

The crowd screamed even more loudly, and a cheer went up, beginning at the back of the room. "Flirts, Flirts, Flirts, Flirts!"

Billy went onstage and held his arms out, gazing into the audience, and the crowd's emotions reached an even higher peak.

"H-2-O-ville?" Erin shouted, trying to make herself heard.

"Waterville!" Emma yelled in her ear, having figured it out.

"Oh!" Erin yelled back.

"*Now!*" Billy shouted, dropping his arms, and the rest of the band charged onto the stage.

Pres had taken advantage of the few minutes in the holding area to strip off his shirt—it was incredibly hot in the club—and he got a bunch of wolf whistles as he took up his position with his bass.

Emma turned to Pres and gave him a

dazzling grin. *I don't blame them for whistling,* she thought. *He is great-looking!*

Billy looked at the other members of the band. "'Dreams of Home'!" he yelled. "Triple time! Like we practiced!"

Everyone looked surprised for a split second, because the Flirts invariably opened with "Love Junkie." But when Billy launched into the red-hot guitar riff that opened "Dreams of Home," Emma knew he was absolutely right—it was the perfect song to start out their set.

Together, Billy and Pres sang the first few verses. But instead of the song's usual warm emotional feel, the stepped-up tempo gave it unique urgency that matched the mood of the crowd.

I've traveled far from where I started
Didn't know just where I'd end.
I met a lot of folks along the way
Some that I'd call friends.

But I just kept on keeping on
Restless as a rolling stone.

Until the day I found this island
And I knew that I was home.

Home is where the heart is
Home is where you're loved
Home is where you make your
dreams come true
Dreams of home, dreams of you.

It's all about Sunset Island, Emma thought as she sang the chorus with Sam and Erin. *It's all about the place I love.* She looked stage right and saw Kurt standing there in the wings, bopping to the music. *And he's the one I love most of all.*

At the end of the first chorus, where there usually was a soft, melodic instrumental bridge that Jay played on piano, Pres pulled on an electric guitar, and he and Billy launched into a dueling-guitars trade of smoking guitar solos.

Sam, Erin, and Emma all began to whoop and holler at the end of the section. Kurt was doing the same thing from offstage.

No one could hear, though, because the

crowd was whooping and hollering even louder than they were.

Then Billy and Pres leaned toward the mike to begin the second verse.

> Now, I have loved and lost before
> Didn't know I'd hurt so bad.
> And I have had some fine—

And then the sound went dead.

There was nothing. No singing, and no guitar. Jay continued to play for a couple of moments, but stopped when he realized there was nothing coming out of his monitor. Only Jake, the drummer, kept on going. But finally Jake too realized that the band had lost its sound system.

"What the hell?" Sam said out loud, but no one besides the band heard her, because the backup singers' mike had gone completely dead as well.

The crowd was equally stunned into silence.

At that moment a voice came through a bullhorn from the back of the club.

"This is the Waterville Fire Department. This club is now in violation of local occupancy-limit laws," the voice boomed out. "We're closing it down for the night! Please leave in an orderly fashion through all exits, including emergency exits. Thank you!"

"I can't believe it," Billy said, turning to the band. "I just can't believe—"

But his words were drowned out by a barrage of boos that came up from the crowd.

"Thank you for your cooperation," the voice repeated. "Please leave in an orderly fashion through all exits, including emergency exits. Thank you!"

The crowd continued to boo, and many people hissed loudly.

Emma looked around at the band. There was really nothing they could do.

"Get the band off the stage!" the voice ordered. Emma could barely make out the uniformed man who was speaking. He seemed to be surrounded by a phalanx of other fire officials, and what looked like police.

"That's our cue," Billy said, his voice full

of resignation. He picked up his guitar and started to lead the band backstage. But this seemed to incense the crowd even more—the booing and catcalling got even louder.

Someone threw an empty beer bottle, which clanged against the front edge of the stage but fortunately didn't explode. The catcalling and yelling reached a deafening level.

"Let's get out of here," Billy said to his bandmates as soon as they reached the wings. Kurt grabbed Emma's hand, and they all hurried out one of the emergency exits of the club, emerging onto Front Street. There was a fire marshall and a slew of police cars parked in front.

A few patrons were making their way out the front door, but not many.

"This club must be clear in five minutes!" The band could hear the amplified voice from within. "This club is in violation of fire laws!"

"This is a nightmare," Jake said, shaking his head.

"I guess we can't blame this one on Diana," Sam said.

Emma held tightly to Kurt's hand as they watched the crowd slowly empty out of the club. Some patrons made nasty remarks to the police officers who were standing by their cars, and one guy carrying a beer gave the cops the finger, but the police just stood there stoically, and no real trouble started.

"I feel like I should have done something to prevent this," Kurt told Emma.

"There wasn't anything you could have done!" Emma exclaimed. "It wasn't your fault that the club let in too many people."

"Yeah, well, that's still how I feel," Kurt said grimly.

Shelly Plotkin was one of the last people out of the club. When he spotted the band, he ran right over to them, grinning wildly and waving. He was as animated as any of them had ever seen him, and Shelly was normally an animated kind of guy.

"Awesome," he chortled. "Just like the Fillmore in the sixties. Totally awesome!"

"We didn't play but a half a song," Pres said.

"Aw, who cares?" Shelly asked, his grin wider. "There's always another day. I could tell you guys were going to kick some major-league bootie, too. Well, that's rock and roll for you!"

Emma shot a look at Billy, who was standing next to Carrie, holding her hand. She was whispering in his ear, and he had a grim look on his face.

I know what he's thinking, Emma thought sadly. *He's thinking so far we're oh-for-two, and that's a terrible start. We've got only two more chances to impress Shelly with the music.*

Just two. That's not many at all.

"Ummmmm," Emma purred as Kurt nuzzled her neck.

"You like?" Kurt asked.

"I like," Emma acknowledged. "A lot."

"I'll do it again," Kurt whispered, and he did. Then he kissed Emma gently, and Emma returned the kiss with all her heart.

It was about one o'clock in the morning,

a few hours after the Up Front fiasco, and while the rest of the group and Shelly were out getting something to eat at an all-night diner on Elm Street, Kurt and Emma had walked all the way up to the Colby College campus.

Once there, they had climbed another huge hill behind the theater building, arriving at a water tower at the top of the hill. Then Kurt had led Emma up a ladder to the very top of the tower, where they now sat together in the bright moonlight.

"Who told you about this place?" Emma asked as Kurt continued to nuzzle her neck.

"A guy at Up Front," Kurt said softly.

"Quit it," Emma warned him, "or I'll have to kiss you."

"Promises, promises," Kurt said huskily, and Emma turned her mouth to his.

"What a night," she sighed when the kiss was over. "Unbelievable."

"No kidding," Kurt replied. "I keep thinking I should have—"

"I told you," Emma interrupted, "there was nothing you could have done. The club shouldn't have sold so many tickets. It's their fault—they got greedy."

"You think Shelly is mad?" Kurt asked.

"Not at all," Emma told him. "He thought it was cool." She shook her head. "I really, really don't like him. I might as well just admit it."

"Because he's a phony," Kurt said. He tickled Emma in the ribs. "You're not used to having to suck up to anyone, are you?"

"Neither are you," Emma pointed out.

"That's true," Kurt agreed. "But, hey, it's not my band. And I sure don't blame Billy and Pres for wanting a shot at the brass ring."

"I want it for them so much," Emma said fervently. "I really do."

Kurt looked at her, a bemused expression on his face.

He sees right through me, Emma thought quickly. *He always can.*

"Okay, *I* want it, too," she confessed. "But I won't be with the Flirts forever. I mean, it's not *my* dream. It's theirs."

"I know what my dream is," Kurt said

softly, running his fingers along Emma's neck until she shivered.

"What's that?" Emma whispered.

He answered her with a passionate kiss. "I can't believe I almost lost you," he said when he came up for air.

"I can't even imagine my life without you," Emma told him, her mixed feelings of a few days before seeming very far away. "I don't want to."

"Me either."

She pulled just far enough away from him to look into his eyes. "But when the summer ends . . ."

"Shhh," he whispered, reaching for her.

"But what will happen?" Emma asked, her eyes searching his.

"Emma," Kurt said in a steady voice, "you and I have been through so much together. There is nothing that is going to break us up now. Nothing."

"You mean that?" Emma asked hopefully.

"You know I do," Kurt said, gently brushing a lock of hair off her face.

"Even if we aren't together? Geographically, I mean?"

"No matter what," Kurt promised, and he pulled her into his embrace.

After they had kissed for a long time, Emma laid her head on Kurt's chest. She could feel the rapid beating of his heart. "I'm so happy," she murmured.

"Me, too."

"Do you think the Flirts will get their record deal?"

"I hope so," Kurt said. "Because if they don't . . ." His voice trailed off.

Emma pulled away and looked at him. "What?"

"Maybe I shouldn't say anything. . . ."

"Tell me!" Emma insisted.

"Well, Pres told me that if it doesn't work out with Polimar this time, he's thinking about moving on."

"No!" Emma exclaimed.

"He's talking about going back to Tennessee," Kurt said. "To Nashville."

"You're kidding."

"That's what he said," Kurt maintained.

"He told me he knows a lot of people there, and he could get session work."

"But what about the Flirts?" Emma asked, her voice rising. "And what about Sam?"

Kurt shrugged. "I don't know."

Billy would be devastated, Emma thought. *After all, he and Pres are really the heart and soul of the Flirts. But no one would be as devastated as Sam.*

No one.

EIGHT

"Emma, are you on drugs?" Sam asked her friend. Emma was going over the dance break for "Love Junkie" by herself in one corner of their motel room. She'd just done it for the fifth time.

"I'm practicing, that's all," Emma said. "Is there something wrong with that?"

"But you know that dance break like you know your own name!" Erin said as she stretched out on one of the double beds.

"I just want to make sure the show is perfect tonight," Emma said, executing a double spin move. "Why don't you two practice with me? Come on, get up, there's lots of room."

It was the next afternoon, and the Flirts

had arrived in Lewiston for their next gig. Billy and Pres were at Lewiston's small airport, waiting for the arrival of Sly, while Kurt was at the L.A. Club (for Lewiston-Auburn; Auburn was the town closest to Lewiston) setting up and making sure security arrangements for that night were in good shape. No one wanted a repeat of the debacle in Waterville. Jay and Jake had gone to check out the town.

Which left Emma, Sam, Erin, and Carrie at the motel. Erin was sitting cross-legged on one bed, painting her fingernails. Sam was next to her, reading a show business gossip magazine. On the other bed Carrie was sprawled out reading a book.

I wish I could tell Sam what Kurt told me about Pres, Emma thought as she danced around the motel room. *But I can't! I gave Kurt my word. So I can't even tell her why I'm up here practicing again, and why I want them to practice with me! If the Flirts don't get the deal, Pres might actually leave Sunset Island. And that would be so horrible for Sam. So horrible!*

"There'd be lots of room if we were all

midgets, Emma. Uh, I know you may not have noticed," Erin said as she carefully screwed the top back onto her bottle of red nail polish, "but there isn't room enough for the three of us to stand up at the same time, much less dance."

"Besides, we've done that routine for real a zillion times," Sam said as she serenely turned the page in her magazine. "Oh my God, it says here that Brad Pitt might be secretly married!"

"I can't keep a secret," Erin said, and grinned.

"How much did they pay you for that article?" Sam teased.

"Not enough," Erin joked back.

"I just think we could improve," Emma insisted, trying to get her friends to focus. She stopped dancing and put her hands on her hips.

"What's gotten into you?" Erin asked her, blowing on the wet polish on her nails.

"Nothing," Emma maintained. "I just want us to be great." She looked over at Sam.

All this has to do with you, she thought. *I wish I could just tell you!*

"Don't you want us to be great?"

"We *are* great," Sam said, not lifting her eyes from the magazine. "So Brad was seen with some babe in this ritzy shop and she bought what looked like a wedding dress," she reported. "I am so bummed—he told me he was saving himself for me!"

"Pres is cuter than Brad Pitt," Erin said with a grin. "A lot cuter."

"You think?" Sam said mischievously, finally looking up. "I'd have to see them side by side to be sure, wearing nothing but, oh, a cute pair of baggy shorts—"

"Sam!" Emma exploded. "Aren't you ever serious about anything?"

Everyone looked at Emma. Even Carrie looked up from her book, since the outburst was so out of character for her friend.

"Something's wrong," Carrie stated.

"Nothing's wrong!" Emma insisted, her voice a little strident.

"Oh, I get it!" Erin said, swinging her legs around on the bed. "It's about Sly, right? You're worried about Sly!"

"We're all worried about Sly, Em," Carrie said. "It's okay."

Emma plopped down in the only chair in the room. "I wasn't thinking about Sly just now," she admitted. "Not just now."

"What, then?" Carrie asked.

"I . . ." Emma looked over at Sam. "Never mind. Forget about it."

"I hate it when you have secrets!" Sam cried. "You know I live for gossip!"

"It's . . . Never mind," Emma said. She looked out the window at the beautiful, sunny day. "Sly should be here soon," she said, wanting to change the subject.

"We should talk about it," Carrie suggested, putting a bookmark in her book.

"What's to talk about?" Erin said. "There's nothing we can do but be his buds. Which is exactly what I'm planning to do."

"You don't know him," Sam pointed out. "He left the band before you came in."

"What difference does that make?" Erin asked, shaking her blond curls out of her eyes. "He's a human being, isn't he?"

"Aren't you worried about his dying?"

Carrie asked, looking at Erin closely. "Because I sure am."

"Of course," Erin answered. "But there's nothing I can do about it except be there for him."

"It doesn't seem real," Sam reflected in a low voice. "I mean, we can talk about Sly's dying, and in my mind I know it's real, but . . ."

"But a part of your mind still doesn't believe it, right?" Emma asked. "That's how I feel."

"Right," Sam agreed with a sigh. She shivered. "It's so scary."

"And he's so young," Emma added. She looked out the window again. "Do you ever think about dying? I mean, about yourself dying?"

"Oh, too morbid!" Sam cried. "Yuck! Forget it! I'm living forever!"

"Sometimes I think about my parents dying," Carrie admitted. "Like if my dad looks really tired, I'll think about him getting old and . . ." She let the rest of her sentence trail off. "But then it's too awful and scary to think about, so I just shut it off."

"Yeah," Erin agreed. "When my father was in that fire, I was so scared. I don't know how I would have handled it if—"

"You guys, I hate this conversation," Sam said, throwing herself back on the bed. "Let's talk about guys, or food, or anything else!"

Just then a couple of knocks sounded on the door of their room. Sam sat up quickly, her face pale.

Emma looked around at everyone. "We can do this," she said quietly. Then she got up and opened the door.

It was Sly, and Billy stood by his side, holding him lightly by the arm. Sly was dressed in blue jeans, a long-sleeved white T-shirt, and the Flirting With Danger tour jacket that everyone had chipped in to buy him.

Sly was so skinny that the clothes just hung on him, as if they were draped over a sagging clothesline. All the bones in his face stuck out, and his eyes looked huge, sunk deep into their sockets.

He looks so awful, Emma thought as she took in his appearance. Even though she thought she had prepared herself mentally for this moment, she was still shocked. *He looks like he's going to die.*

"Hey," Sly said, his voice strong, "what's up, everyone?"

A smile spread across Emma's face. She reached out and hugged him hard. "Oh, Sly . . ." She buried her head in his shoulder. "I am so glad to see you!"

Carrie and Sam rushed over to him. Erin hung back a bit. First Carrie, then Sam eagerly hugged the Flirts' former drummer. He wrapped his skinny arms around them and hugged them back.

"Wow, the three of you look great," Sly said, his pale face beaming with happiness.

"Sly," Billy said, "I want you to meet our new backup singer, Erin Kane."

"Not Diana?" Sly asked. "I mean, what are the Flirts without Diana's charm?"

Everyone laughed.

"Good to finally meet you, Sly," Erin

said, coming forward. She held out her hand, which Sly took.

"You're the one who's going out with Jake?" he asked Erin. She nodded.

Sly smiled at her. "He's a lucky guy."

"Well, thanks," Erin said lightly. "I'll take that as a compliment."

They chatted for a while longer. When the flow of conversation finally slowed, Sly asked, "Anyone want to go on a mission with me?"

"Where to?" Carrie queried.

"Into town. I'd drive myself, but . . ." His voice trailed off.

"Sly can't see so great," Billy hastened to explain. "Virus in his eyes. I'd drive him, but I want to go over to the club."

"I'll take you, Sly," Emma volunteered.

"Drop me at the club?" Billy asked as he wrapped his arm around Carrie.

"Sure," Emma agreed.

"See you later, gorgeous," Billy told Carrie, giving her a quick kiss.

Sly smiled. "Glad to see you two are still an item."

"Forever," Billy promised.

Sly looked over at Sam. "And how about you and Pres?"

"That's forever, too," Sam said. "At least, I hope so."

Not unless we get a record deal, Emma thought, feeling anxious all over again.

Sly looked around at his friends. "This is . . . this is really great, man," he said quietly. "Really great."

"It's called cytomegalovirus," Sly explained as he sat in the passenger seat of the van.

Emma, who was behind the wheel, had just dropped Billy off at the L.A. Club. She was now heading toward downtown Lewiston.

"How bad are your eyes?" Emma asked him, her own eyes on the road.

"Pretty bad," Sly admitted, his voice matter-of-fact. "But then again, so is the rest of me."

He's not kidding, Emma thought. *He's got purplish spots on his face—lesions from Kaposi's sarcoma—and he's so, so skinny. And my guess is he's dressed the way he is because he's cold all the time. It must be so horrible!*

Emma glanced at him. "It means a lot to all of us that you came."

"Not as much as it does to me," Sly told her.

"So, where are we going?" Emma asked.

Sly was silent for a moment, then said lightly, "I want to find a church."

"A church?" Emma echoed.

Sly's voice got a little more serious. "I've been praying a lot lately," he said. "Can you blame me, Emma?"

"No," Emma said, biting her lower lip. "I can't blame you at all."

"It helps," Sly said affirmatively. "For some reason, it really helps."

"Do you care what kind of church?" Emma asked as she scanned both sides of the road, looking for a church, any church.

"Nope," Sly said. "Church, synagogue, whatever. I don't care. I don't think He cares much, either, if you catch my drift."

Emma saw a white steeple ahead to her left, about a hundred yards away. "There's one," she said.

"Please stop, okay?" Sly asked her.

Emma pulled off the road and into the nearly deserted church parking lot.

"You want to come in?" Sly asked her.

"Sure," Emma agreed, not wanting Sly to have to go in alone. The two of them got out, Emma helping Sly, and they walked up to the church.

The front door was open, and the two of them went inside. Just past the front vestibule was the sanctuary, a smallish room with about twenty rows of hard pews on either side.

Sly slid into one of the pews, and Emma went in and sat next to him. *I can't even remember the last time I went to a church service,* she realized. *My mother occasionally goes, but that's only because it's a Beacon Hill high-society church, and she's there so she can be seen by the right people.*

She took a quick glance at Sly, but he'd already closed his eyes. So she closed her own.

God, Emma prayed, *I try to be the best person I can be. I'm not perfect, and sometimes I don't do the best I can, but a lot of the time I really do try. I try to be a true friend to my friends.*

Sly needs Your help. So I'm going to pray as if everything depends on You, and act as if everything depends on me.

Please keep him alive as long as he needs to be. And . . . and please help me to be there for him in every way.

Emma kept her eyes shut for a long time, focusing on the quiet, the stillness, the peace of the room she was in. When she finally opened them, Sly was looking at her, a tender smile on his face.

"You okay?" he asked her.

Emma nodded, even though her eyes were shiny with tears.

"Me, too," Sly said. "Now, let's rock and roll!"

"Fabulous!" Shelly Plotkin cried, pumping Billy's hand over and over. "Totally fabuloso, my man."

"Thanks, Shelly," Billy said modestly, taking a gulp of mineral water. "It means a lot, coming from you."

"Now, that's rock!" Shelly said meaningfully. "That's rock! I kid you not!"

It was about midnight that same night. The Flirts had just finished their gig at the L.A. Club and were gathered backstage in the dressing room.

For the first time on this tour, everything had gone perfectly. There had been a good-sized crowd, there were no problems with the local fire department, and the audience had loved them. In fact, the Flirts had been brought back for two encores—the second one a version of Bruce Springsteen's classic song "Born to Run" that they hadn't played since the big East Coast tour, and which Billy had been holding in reserve. That night they had played it.

Sly had watched the entire show from the wings, and he'd already told them he'd loved every minute of it. He had added that he would have done one drum solo differently than Jake had, and Jake had replied that he'd heard that Sly was a drummer in a class by himself.

I was a little nervous that Jake and Sly wouldn't get along, Emma thought, *but the two of them have already become fast friends.* She looked over at Sly, who was sitting near the door, Jake next to him. She caught his eye. He nodded at her, and winked almost imperceptibly.

"I'm telling you people, this is the start of something big," Shelly went on. "Major!"

Emma, who was sitting on the dressing room couch between Sam and Erin, turned to smile at Sam. *We did it!* she thought happily. *He'll give the Flirts a deal now. He has to!*

"So, you really liked us?" Sam asked eagerly, her eyes shining.

"*Liked* isn't the word," Shelly said. "Loved. Knocked out. Totally! I'll have a dyno-mite report for New York tomorrow. Absolutely dyno-mite!"

"Cool," Pres said, reaching for an icy Coke from the cooler beside him. "We're lookin' forward to your decision."

"Yes, indeedy," Shelly chortled, scratching his chest absentmindedly. "Cody Leete's gonna love you!"

Cody Leete? Emma asked herself. *Who in the world is Cody Leete?*

At that moment Kurt came into the dressing room. "The stuff's all in the van," he reported.

"Roadies never get enough credit in our biz," Shelly told Kurt.

"Thanks," Kurt said with a grin.

Emma got up and gave Kurt a hug.

"And thanks to you, too!" Kurt said with a laugh, his arms still around Emma.

"You mentioned somebody named Cody Leete," Billy said easily. "Who's he?"

"Oh!" Shelly laughed uncomfortably. "Cody! You must know about Cody!"

Billy looked at Pres, who shrugged.

"Never heard of him, Shelly," Billy replied, his voice still very light.

"Ditto," Pres drawled.

"Oh!" Shelly laughed again. "He'll be flying in for your Portland show. While I'm back in New York. Gotta scout a band at CBGB. Cool club."

Emma got a sick feeling in her stomach.

"Cody Leete," Billy repeated. "You never mentioned him. . . ."

"Great guy, just a great guy!" Shelly

said, seemingly trying to be as enthusiastic as possible.

"I thought you were the main guy," Sly said.

"Oh, yeah," Shelly assured him. "I am. But Cody's the *main* main guy!"

Everyone stared at him.

"Hey, you guys are the best," Shelly pointed out, "totally the best. You've got nothing to worry about. Cody'll *love* you!"

"Shelly," Billy said, "you told us that if you wanted to, you could make the deal."

Shelly got a little huffy. "It's corporate, man," he told them. "There's nothin' I can do about it."

"How come you never said anything about Cody Leete before?" Sly challenged, his voice thin but full of steel.

Shelly looked at him helplessly.

"Whatever," Billy said quickly. "We'll play for anyone."

Emma looked around the room. The atmosphere had completely changed. Two minutes earlier, the mood in the dressing room had been jubilant. Now it was downright somber.

So, Emma thought, *it's all going to come down to one show, to the opinion of some man we've never even met before.*

She looked at Sly, whose face had grown even paler after his comment, and then she looked over at Sam, who didn't even know the terrible secret about Pres.

And everything, Emma thought, *absolutely everything depends on the last show.*

NINE

"Do you think the new guy will like us?" Emma asked Sam and Carrie, who were standing on either side of her as the ferry bound for Sunset Island sliced through the slight chop of Casco Bay.

"Who?" Sam asked.

"Cody Leete, of course," Emma said as she stared out at the water. "The guy from Polimar."

"Oh, how could he help it?" Sam asked. "We're the greatest."

"I hope he agrees," Emma replied.

"All I care about is whether he has great taste in music and loves the Flirts."

"Amen," Emma breathed fervently.

It was the next morning, around ten

o'clock. The band had left Lewiston bright and early, bound for their next gig in Portland. But instead of just pulling into Portland and spending the day hanging around and waiting for their gig, Billy had announced a surprise just as they reached the Maine Turnpike exit that led to downtown Portland.

"We're going home for the day," he'd announced. "Graham Perry called to say he's throwing a small party for us at his house. Then we're catching the five o'clock ferry back for our sound check. It should give us enough time."

Everyone cheered with happiness at Billy's announcement. Although the band had been away from the island for only a few days, they looked forward to the chance to chill out before their all-important gig that night in front of the unknown and somehow very scary Polimar exec Cody Leete.

So Sam, Emma, and Carrie were hanging out together on the front deck of the ferry as Sunset Island slowly came into view on the horizon, while the rest of the gang was inside the vessel.

"It was so rotten of Shelly not to tell us about Cody in the first place," Emma said as she brushed some windblown hair off her cheek.

"Sometimes it seems like the closer to a record deal you guys get, the more elusive the whole thing is," Carrie said.

"To dream the impossible dream!" Sam sang out.

"It's *not* impossible," Emma insisted, worrying for the zillionth time about what Kurt had told her about Pres. "It's going to happen."

"Billy's feeling pretty good about everything," Carrie reported.

"He should be," Sam snorted. "The two of you shared a room last night!"

Carrie blushed slightly. It was true. Instead of her sleeping in the same room as the other girls, Billy had come to Carrie's shared room just after they got back to the motel to tell her that he'd arranged for another motel room, at his own expense, just for him and Carrie.

"Was it wonderful?" Emma asked softly.

"Yes," Carrie admitted, a happy smile on her face. "That's the right word."

Would I feel that way if I slept with Kurt? Emma wondered. *Am I missing out on something? But what good is the promise I made to myself to wait until I'm married if I change my mind just because it would be fun? On the other hand, maybe waiting is ridiculous. Maybe if you really love someone you should—*

"Emma-bo-bemma!" Sam called, tapping her on the shoulder.

"Huh? What?" Emma asked, startled out of her reverie.

"I asked you a question," Sam said regally.

"I was thinking," Emma said.

"I hope you were thinking about how you and your hunk o' burning love are doing," Sam repeated. "Because that's what I asked you about."

Emma blushed. "Really good," she reported.

"Lots of details," Sam quipped to Carrie.

"That's Emma Cresswell for you." Carrie grinned.

Sam nudged Emma in the ribs. "You gonna go for the gusto?"

Emma shook her head. "I don't think so."

"Well, in a way I'm glad," Sam confessed. "I couldn't stand to be the only nineteen-year-old virgin on Sunset Island."

"You know, Sam," Emma said softly, "I was thinking that maybe this tour would be the time you and Pres, well, you know . . ."

"Nah," Sam replied. "It'd be too distracting. Wrong time, wrong place."

Carrie laughed. "I can't believe my ears!"

"It is funny," Emma commented as the ferry approached the dock. "I never thought you'd put work before guys."

"See, the two of you constantly underestimate me," Sam said with dignity. "I happen to be a professional."

"Professional guy-watcher," Carrie joked.

"Well, yeah, that, too," Sam agreed. "I look but do not touch!"

Emma glanced over at her friend. "You really love Pres, don't you?"

"I think so," Sam said. "Not that I know what love is, mind you."

"But you'd be hurt if he . . . moved away from the island or something, right?" Emma asked carefully.

Sam stared at her. "What are you talking about?"

"Nothing!" Emma said quickly. "I was just wondering. Because you joke around about guys so much—"

"Well, come on, that's just me, Em," Sam said. "You know that!"

"Right, I do," Emma agreed, shifting her gaze to the gulls wheeling above the boat.

"Pres is the best thing that ever happened to me," Sam confessed in a low voice. "Other than meeting the two of you, that is."

"Sunset Island, Maine," called a voice over the ferry's loudspeaker. "Return trips to the mainland leave every two hours, on the half hour. Have a pleasant stay."

"Thanks for the compliment," Carrie said lightly.

"Emma," Sam began, "if there's something you're not telling me—"

"No, nothing," Emma lied. "I was just wondering about the two of you, that's all."

"Well, wonder no more," Sam said. "I'm crazy about the boy. Hey, I hope they have a lot of food at this bash, because I am starved!"

"Welcome!" Claudia Templeton said as she opened the back gate to Emma, Jane Hewitt, and the Hewitt kids.

It was later that afternoon, and the party that Graham was throwing for the Flirts was in full swing. Emma had decided to stop back at the Hewitts' house to get a dress for the party. She had found that the whole family was extremely excited about the party. Katie had already tried on every single outfit she owned, until she'd finally decided on pink bike shorts and a pink and white ruffled T-shirt.

Emma had chosen her outfit carefully, too. She wanted to look casual, but at the same time she wanted to dazzle Kurt. Finally she'd chosen a white off-the-shoulder leotard, which she wore with a casual long white cotton skirt. On her feet she wore little white ballet flats, and she threaded a narrow white ribbon through her hair. After adding tiny pearl earrings, some brown mascara, bronzer, and lip gloss, she sprayed herself all over with Sunset Magic perfume.

Well, this will have to do, she told herself as she packed her new white bathing suit with the apple-green piping around the bust and legs. *I hope Kurt likes it.* She threw the matching coverup in her bag, too.

It's the last outfit I bought before my mother cancelled all my credit cards, she recalled. *I'd better enjoy it.*

As Emma walked into the huge, lavish backyard, she noticed that about fifty people had already arrived, and about half of them were cavorting in the swimming pool. All of the Flirts except Sly were engaged in a heated water volleyball game. Emma knew Sly was resting back at the Flirts' house.

She took in the happy sight of her friends batting the white ball back and forth over the net. Sam had on a teeny pink bikini, and Carrie had on her navy blue tank suit. Kurt looked darling in baby-blue surfer jams, the drops of water on his tanned and muscular chest glinting in the sun.

Next to the pool, Graham and Claudia had put out a fabulous spread. There were six-foot-long heros, iced shrimp, cold roast chicken, nearly every kind of cold drink you could imagine, potato salad and coleslaw chilled over ice, and magnificent floral arrangements with attached multicolored helium balloons flying in the breeze.

"Where's Ian?" Ethan asked, trying to look casual.

Emma looked around. "Over there," she said when she spotted him. Ian was with Becky and Allie Jacobs and the rest of his band, the Zits, sitting under a huge sycamore tree.

"See ya!" Ethan said, heading off.

"I'm coming, too!" Wills said, trotting after him.

"Can I go swimming?" Katie asked her mom.

"Sure," Jane said. "Let's go over to the cabana and I'll help you change."

"Make yourselves at home," Claudia told Emma kindly. "Excuse me, I've got to check on the caterer in the kitchen."

"That was fast," Emma commented a couple of minutes later as Jane strolled back over to her, minus Katie.

"Oh, Katie insists she's old enough to change by herself," Jane said with a smile. "She's getting very independent."

"Soon she'll be *my* au pair!" Emma replied, matching Jane's grin. "Want something to drink?"

"The lemonade looks great," Jane said.

Emma poured them both a glass and handed one to Jane.

"So, Emma the rock star," Jane said, sipping her lemonade, "how's life on the road?"

"Fine," Emma replied. *I can't begin to get into the whole thing,* she thought. *Although actually Jane would probably be very understanding.* "So, how's my, uh, replacement doing?"

Jane laughed. "Irene? It's been great. I've even learned a few things about parenting!" She eyed the buffet. "Want to get some food?"

"Sure," Emma replied, and the two of them walked over to the overloaded table.

"This looks fantastic," Jane said. She took a plate, put a piece of the hero on it, and then added some coleslaw and potato salad. "So much for low-fat eating," she added ruefully, looking at her plate.

"Do the kids like her?" Emma asked.

"Like her?" Jane laughed again. "They love her! I've never seen them so polite."

"Oh, well, that's nice," Emma said, trying hard to sound enthusiastic. But inside she couldn't help feeling hurt. *Maybe I'm not the au pair that Jane really wants,* she thought, feeling insecure. *Maybe Jane is going to decide she wants someone else. Then what will I do? I'll never find another job.*

"Oh, don't look so worried," Jane said with a grin, taking a bite of potato salad. "You'll have your job back tomorrow. No problem."

Emma smiled. "Thanks," she said sincerely.

"Oh!" Jane said, reaching into her pocketbook and taking out an envelope. "A letter came for you from your dad."

Emma took the letter from Jane's hand. "Thanks," she said again.

"My pleasure," Jane said. "Listen, I'm going to go sit with Dan Jacobs over there—he's by himself. I'll see you later. Bye!" She gave Emma a quick wave and headed over to the picnic table where Sam's boss was sitting.

As soon as Jane left Emma's side Ethan and Wills Hewitt got up from where they were sitting under the sycamore tree and ran at top speed over to Emma, who was still standing by the buffet table.

"You've got to do something!" Ethan exclaimed, grabbing Emma's arm. "She's killing us!"

"Your mother?" Emma asked, puzzled.

"No!" Wills cried, grabbing Emma's other arm. "Mrs. Wentworth!"

"Irene," Ethan sneered. "Except she won't let us call her Irene. We have to call her, ahem, 'Mrs. Wentworth.' Gag me."

"Double gag me, I hate her guts," Wills lamented. "She stinks."

"But your mother says—" Emma began, surprised at what the kids were saying.

"She's got Mom snowed," Ethan broke in, his voice confidential. He darted a glance over at his mother to make sure that Jane wasn't watching him. "She bosses us around all the time, and then sucks up to Mom."

"I hate her guts," Wills repeated.

"But she's a famous expert!" Emma said.

"You try living with her," Ethan complained, reaching for a cherry tomato on the buffet table and popping it directly into his mouth.

"Yeah," Wills agreed. "She'd kill Ethan for grabbing that tomato just now. I think she eats little kids for breakfast."

"She's got all these rules," Ethan went on. "Like we have to use a certain fork for certain foods. We have to fold our napkins in a certain way. We even have to stand up when Mom enters the room!"

"But your mother told me that you love her!" Emma exclaimed.

"So wrong," Ethan said.

"But your mom is usually so in touch with you guys."

"Listen, this time Mom has completely lost it," Ethan said seriously. "It's like just because this woman is some big famous deal, what she says has to be right."

"I seriously hate her guts," Wills said.

"Yes, I got that," Emma said with a laugh.

"Are you coming back soon?" Wills asked plaintively.

Emma nodded. "Tomorrow."

"Told you," Ethan said to Wills.

"I knew that," Wills replied with dignity. "Hooray for Emma!"

"Shhh!" Ethan instructed his brother as he saw Jane looking over at them. He gave his mother a wave, and she waved back.

"Where's Mrs. Wentworth now?" Emma asked, bemused by this whole conversation.

"Home," Ethan confided, snatching up another cherry tomato. "Probably writing up our behavior grades or something."

"Oh, you're exaggerating," Emma scoffed.

"No! She has a big red chart on the wall with our behavior grades on it!" Wills told her. "I'm glad you're coming back."

"Me, too," Ethan said. "Hey, Emma, could you do us a favor?"

"Of course," Emma answered. "If I can."

"Don't go on any more band trips, all right?" Ethan begged. "Or if you do . . . take us along!"

"Quiet! Quiet!"

Graham Perry was clinking a spoon against the side of a bottle of juice, trying to get everyone's attention. The party had spread out all over the backyard, so it took a little while.

Finally, though, everyone shut up and turned their eyes and ears to the world-famous rock star, who was standing over by the buffet table. He was wearing cutoff jeans and a blue T-shirt, and he looked much younger than he actually was.

Claudia edged up next to him and looked at him, her eyes bright, her face glowing. Emma thought they looked almost like teenagers again.

"I wanted to say a few words," Graham began, the Maine sun shining brightly off his long, thick hair.

Everyone listened expectantly. It wasn't often they got to hear a speech from Graham Perry.

"I still remember," Graham continued, "when I was starting out. I was just a kid, playing these little dives on the Jersey shore. I wasn't making any money. And then, one night, some record exec was in the crowd. After the show he came up to me in my dressing room—it wasn't a dressing room, really, it was a hole in the wall—and he said the words I'd always dreamed of: 'Kid, have you ever thought about a recording contract?'

"I was so excited," Graham went on. "So I know just how Billy and the whole band feel right now. The pressure's on them. There's a big gig tonight. But there's always gonna be pressure, and there's always gonna be heat, and there's always gonna be someone to say you can't do it, guys.

"I know you can do it, Flirts. You've got what it takes. You've paid your dues," Graham concluded. "We'll be with you all the way. *I'm* with you all the way."

Everyone broke into applause.

"Thanks, Graham," Billy said sincerely. "You don't know how much that means to us."

Everyone applauded again.

Emma, who was standing holding hands with Kurt as Graham spoke, looked over at Billy and Carrie together, and at Sam and Pres together, and she thought she saw a tear in the corner of Billy's eye.

A chant went up from the people in the crowd, "Flirts, Flirts, Flirts!"

Carrie whispered something in Billy's ear, and he put his arm around her and hugged her tight.

"This is great, huh?" Kurt said, leaning close to her.

"The best," Emma replied.

And at that moment Emma felt very, very proud to be a part of something a lot bigger than she was.

"It's going to happen tonight," Kurt said. "I just know it is."

"I hope you're right," Emma said, glancing at Pres, who was standing with his arm around Sam. "For everyone. And especially for Sam."

"You didn't tell her, did you?" Kurt whispered.

Emma shook her head.

No, I didn't tell her, Emma thought. *It was the hardest thing in the world not to, though. The hardest thing.*

Emma closed the door to the bathroom off Graham Perry's family room. She hadn't had a moment alone since Jane had given her the letter from her father, and she was determined to read it.

Now, finally, she was alone.

She carefully opened the envelope and pulled out a single sheet of her dad's business stationery. Her father's familiar scrawl filled the page.

She sat down on the side of the tub and began to read.

My darling daughter,

What a summer! The last few weeks have been pretty hellish for your father, as you can imagine. The stock market crash hurt me very badly, and then I was very, very upset when I learned what your mother had done to you.

At the time, there was nothing I could do, and I felt awful about that.

I just wanted to tell you, though, that I'm working on it. There's no money that I can give you, unfortunately, but that doesn't mean that I can't change Kat's mind. I've been trying. It's a tough process with your mother, because at first she didn't even want to talk to me. But she's relented a little. I do think that I might need to put her on my staff, seeing as how she's probably the only person in America who *made* money during the crash!

I've told her that what she's done won't work, that it will only make you more rebellious, and that she'll end up pushing you away from her . . . and from me.

Don't tell her, but I think that I'm making some progress with her. The hard part is going to be to get your mother to tell you that she's changed her mind. She doesn't want to lose face, if you know what I mean. So when she does tell you, don't be rough on her.

She did what she thought was right, even if she was wrong. And the greatest thing about being a grown-up, in my opinion, is that you get to change your mind if you want to.

So be good. I think there's going to be some good news really soon.

Love,

Dad

Emma read the letter twice, and by the end of the second time, she was beginning to believe that the letter wasn't just another awful joke by Diana De Witt, but that maybe, actually, possibly, it was true.

TEN

"That's *him*?" Sam asked incredulously, looking at the man sitting on the far side of the dressing room, his head buried in a magazine. She had been in the changing area of the dressing room, putting on her stage outfit, when the Polimar exec had come in and joined the Flirts.

"Uh-huh," Carrie answered softly, not wanting to be overheard. "That's Cody Leete."

"I am not filled with confidence," Emma admitted, looking over at Leete.

It was around nine-forty, and the Flirts were all gathered in the dressing room of the Jack of Clubs, the well-known rock and roll venue on the Portland waterfront, for their final, make-or-break concert of the Maine minitour.

Cody Leete, the Polimar exec who had flown in from New York to make the final decision about the band, was in the dressing room with the Flirts. But where Shelly Plotkin had been ebullient and talkative, Cody was extremely cold and standoffish.

In fact, he'd barely spoken to anyone in the band since his arrival.

"He's old! He looks like he could be my father!" Sam snorted as they watched Leete stand up, straighten his suit, and then walk over to the small bathroom.

"Forty, maybe," Carrie noted, relieved that Leete could not now overhear them.

"Get out of town!" Sam exclaimed. "The dude is pushing fifty at least. I mean, Graham Perry is forty!"

"Well, at least he wears nice clothes," Erin said lamely.

"Please," Sam retorted.

But Erin was right. Where Shelly Plotkin favored loud Hawaiian shirts and jeans, Cody Leete looked like he could have stepped out of any big-city executive suite.

He wore an immaculate and perfectly pressed double-breasted summerweight gray wool suit, a white cotton shirt with French cuffs, and a red-and-blue-striped tie. On his feet were perfectly shined black Italian leather loafers.

All this, together with his gray-flecked medium-length dark hair and the horn-rimmed glasses he wore, made for a totally corporate-looking appearance. He could have been a New York City investment advisor.

"My father wouldn't have that suit in his wardrobe," Emma sniffed. "No character."

Sam laughed. "Trust Emma to put the dude in his place!"

"So what did Kurt say he was like?" Erin asked Emma anxiously. Kurt had picked Cody up at the airport.

Emma sighed. "He said Cody didn't say a single word the whole ride over here."

"A charmer," Sam quipped. "Did he talk to Billy or Pres yet?"

Carrie shook her head. "Nope," she muttered. "Not a word."

"We just have to do our best, that's all,"

Emma said, trying to control her nervousness.

"Maybe you ought to go do your snooty imitation of your mother," Sam suggested to Emma. "That might get him."

"I don't know—he looks pretty cool and collected. I doubt Kat herself could get him to react," Emma said.

Emma thought again about the letter from her father. *If he gets Mother to relent,* Emma thought, *I could pay for the Flirts to do an album myself if I wanted to. Not that they'd ever let me. But maybe I could do something. . . .*

"Listen, this guy is going to hate my latest Samstyles," Sam said, looking down at her stage outfit. "He's seriously conservative!"

Emma looked down at herself, then at Sam and Erin. They had on Sam's latest creation, the one they'd saved for their very last gig: antique pastel lacy bed jackets that bared their stomachs (Sam's bared the most, Erin's bared the least) with short, almost sheer pastel skirts held together by small rhinestone pins. On their feet they wore off-white lace-up ankle boots to which tiny rhinestone pins had been glued.

"We could change into one of our other outfits, I guess," Erin said.

"I don't have any of the others here," Emma said. "Anyway, we are who we are. And I love these outfits," she added loyally. "They're original and fantastic."

Sam smiled at her gratefully. "Did I ever mention how cool you are?"

"Once or twice," Emma replied with a grin.

"Excuse me, you guys," Carrie said, fiddling with one of the cameras slung around her neck. "I'm going out front to get ready for your big entrance."

"When do we go on?" Emma asked.

"Around ten," Carrie replied. "When the warm-up band is finished."

Right then someone from the club staff popped in to tell the Flirts they needed to get ready to go on. And through the thin walls of the dressing room they could hear the violent rock chords and aggressive singing of Goes to Eleven, the power-pop band that had been booked by Jack of Clubs to open for the Flirts.

"Stay out of their mosh pit," Sam advised.

"Don't worry," Carrie answered. "I'll be far away from it."

Carrie left. Emma followed her with her gaze, and then noticed Billy, who was conferring with Pres over by the small card table that held bottles of juice and a small tray of sandwiches. Billy and Pres kept glancing over in Sly Smith's direction. Sly was resting on one of the dressing room couches.

Then Billy and Pres seemed to make a decision. Billy called for the band's attention, and Pres, Jay, Jake, Sly, Erin, Sam, and Emma began to gather around him. Emma sneaked a glance at Cody. He didn't even look up from the magazine he had started to read as soon as he came out of the bathroom.

"You doing okay?" Billy said to Sly as the band's former drummer made his way over to him, slowly but surely.

Emma noticed how pale Sly's face was.

He doesn't look very good, she thought. *He looks really, really tired. Almost white. Even more tired than he looked when he first arrived.*

"Been better, man," Sly said weakly, turning his palms up in a gesture of resignation. His long-sleeved shirt hung on his gaunt figure.

"You can hang back here," Billy said to him.

"Are you kidding?" Sly retorted. His eyes shone with a fire that belied his emaciated condition. "I'm not gonna miss this. I'll be right out there."

"Great," Billy said fervently. Then he turned his attention to Cody Leete.

"Mr. Leete?" Billy called.

Cody looked up slowly from the magazine. "Yes?"

"Could you excuse us for a minute?" Billy asked.

Cody gave Billy an arch look. "Excuse you?" he asked, his voice skeptical and withering.

"Exactly," Billy said. "We'd like a minute alone here, please."

"What, exactly, is the point of this drama?" Cody asked sarcastically.

"So we can prepare," Billy said, his voice matter-of-fact. "We're about to give a performance."

"If you're not ready, you're not ready," Cody remarked cuttingly. But he got to his feet and left the room.

"Jerk," Sam mumbled when he'd left.

"Ignore him," Emma advised, but her stomach was churning. *How are we ever going to get that cold fish to give us a contract?* she worried. She glanced over at Pres. *Please,* she thought, *please don't leave the Flirts just because it all came down to one night with some idiot record executive!*

"Bring back Shelly Plotkin," Erin quipped, and everyone laughed.

"Amen," said Sam fervently.

"Nothin' we can do about him," Pres drawled.

"That's right. We have to ignore him and keep our minds on our set," Jake added.

"You guys are right," Billy said. "We just have to go out there and do our best."

"It's a hometown crowd. That should help," Jay reminded them all.

Everyone nodded. They all were aware that many, many people they knew from Sunset Island had come over on the ferry for the evening's performance. Graham Perry himself had said that he'd try to be there.

"So we just have to do our best," Billy repeated. "We do our best, there's no shame."

"We mess up," Pres said somberly, "and . . ." His voice trailed off. But there was no need for him to finish his sentence.

The band stood quietly in a circle for a moment.

Then Sly spoke. "Do it for me," he said softly. "And do it for you."

There was a pounding at the door of the dressing room.

"Flirts!" a voice yelled. "Let's go, let's go!"

"Let's do it," Billy said quietly. "Let's do it for everyone."

Then they all put their hands out, into the center of the circle, and one by one they piled their hands on top of each other, topped last by bony, shaking fingers, attached to a very thin young man with tears in his eyes.

Emma was practically jumping out of her skin with excitement as she stood by the backup singers' mike behind the band.

They love us, she thought. *It's fantastic!*

The Flirts were nearing the end of their second set.

During the break between sets, the band had rested in the dressing room for about fifteen minutes, and Billy and Pres were obviously psyched.

But Cody had not even shown his face.

I don't know if that's a good sign or a bad sign, Emma thought quickly. And then the thought fled from her mind as Billy prepared to start the next number.

"Let me hear you say *yeah*!" he yelled to the crowd.

"Yeah!" the crowd yelled back.

"Let me hear you say *yeah*!" he shouted.

"Yeah!" the crowd roared, even louder.

"Yeah!" Billy repeated.

"Yeah!" the crowd screamed.

"Yeah!"

"Yeah!"

"Yeah yeah yeah yeah!" Billy howled, and the crowd went totally berserk. Then Jay started the piano portion to Billy Joel's song "The Night the Lights Went Out on Broadway," and the Flirts took it in double time, Jake driving the beat forward on drums.

It was like a rocket taking off. And the crowd loved it. They hooted and applauded crazily as the song snapped to an end.

"Whew!" Billy shouted into his mike.

"Flirts! Flirts! Flirts!" came the spontaneous chant from the back of the room. Flashes from Carrie's camera equipment illuminated the faces of the cheering fans near her.

Please, Cody, Emma thought, *please be listening. Please be listening. For the Flirts. For Pres and Sam. For Sly.*

Then something strange happened.

Jake Fisher, who was at the drum kit just to the left of the backup singers, got up from it and walked right in front of the girls.

What's going on? Emma wondered. She looked at Sam and Erin, who both shrugged helplessly. They were just as stumped as she was.

Billy called for quiet by holding his arms up high. Slowly, very slowly, the packed venue came to a complete hush.

"You know," Billy said conversationally, "this band's been through some tough times. It hasn't been easy. But as tough as it's been for us, it's been a lot tougher for one of our founding members."

Emma got a lump in her throat. *He's talking about Sly,* she realized.

"There's seven of us onstage," Billy continued. "But really, there's eight of us. You know his story. Tonight he's really here. Please give the warmest Maine welcome you can to Mr. Sly Smith!"

The room went bonkers. Slowly Sly walked out onstage, Jake leading him by the arm. Billy went to him and embraced him warmly. So did Pres and Jay.

Sam, Emma, and Erin were all crying softly.

I don't know what Cody's going to think

of this, Emma thought, sniffling. *But I don't care!*

"Billy is awesome," Erin whispered.

And then something even more remarkable happened. Billy and Jake led Sly to the drum kit, and slowly, hesitantly, Sly climbed in behind the drums. Sam, Emma, and Erin all stared, their mouths open in shock. No one had said anything about this beforehand.

The crowd went nuts.

"Okay!" Billy shouted. "Here's our last song!"

It was like a miracle. Some sort of power infused itself into Sly. He banged out the bass drum intro to "Love Junkie," the same song with which the Flirts had opened the show.

You want too much
And you want it too fast
You don't know nothin'
About making love last.
You're a love tornado
That's how you get your kicks
You use me up

And move on to your next fix. . . .
You're just a Love Junkie
A Love Junkie, baby
A Love Junkie
You're driving me crazy. . . .

Sam, Emma, and Erin sang the backup parts as they'd never sung them before. Out of the corner of her eye, Emma could see Sly laughing out loud as he pounded away on the drum kit as though he'd never left it.

And then the song came to a close. Sly gave one last flourish on the snare, crashed the cymbals, and that was it. It was over. A huge roar, by far the loudest of the night, came up from the crowd.

"That's it!" Billy shouted. "See you on the island! We love you!"

He led the band, all of them waving wildly to the crowd, off the stage, and the crowd kept shouting and cheering. "More, more, more, more, more!" the crowd chanted as the Flirts stood offstage, listening to the chanting.

"No encore," Billy decided as the cheering kept going and going. "We're done."

Emma knew what he meant. If they went out onstage again, there was no way they could top the emotion and energy of that last version of "Love Junkie," no matter what they played.

Sly was standing next to Billy, and Sam watched as Billy reached down and took his buddy's hand, as if Sly were a little boy and Billy were his father. Slowly, Sly put his head on Billy's strong shoulder.

Cody Leete walked into the dressing room. The members of the band, who were exhausted, were all sitting together, drinking juice and talking quietly, around or on the single couch. Carrie was back there, too, taking a few pictures.

The conversation ended as Cody Leete strode into the room.

"Flirts, you've got a ways to go," Cody said, his face completely stony.

Emma's heart fell. *It's over,* she thought. *We're done. It's not going to happen. How could he not have loved us, though? Every-*

one else did! She looked around at her bandmates. They were as shocked and stunned by Cody's negative pronouncement as she was.

Billy, naturally, was the first to speak. "Thanks for coming, Cody," he said, his voice quavering a little. "It meant a lot."

"Yeah, man," Pres added, his voice a monotone.

"Thanks for having me," Cody said diffidently. "It was interesting."

"Interesting?" Pres repeated, looking down at the ground.

"Damn," Sam mumbled.

"You're making a big mistake, man!" Sly cried out. Emma guessed he figured he had nothing to lose. "You don't know what you're doing!"

Cody regarded Sly curiously. "That's not true," the record exec replied, his voice still even.

"Well," Sly said, "you're crazy for not signing these guys."

Cody's face never changed. "Who said anything about not signing them?"

"But—"

"All I said is that they have a ways to go," Cody continued, his voice still as neutral as ever. "That doesn't mean they aren't good. Or maybe better than good. We'll see."

Am I losing my mind? Emma wondered. *Is he saying the Flirts are going to get a deal?*

"Show biz rule number one: Don't jump to conclusions. Billy, have your lawyer call my office in the morning, please," Cody said, looking at his watch. "And now you'll have to excuse me. I have to get back to my hotel." With that, he turned and left the room.

Oh my God, Emma thought. *It's happening. It's really, really happening.*

For a second everyone in the room was shocked. Then pandemonium broke loose. People were cheering, slapping each other high fives, hugging. Pres came over and gave Sam a big kiss, which Sam returned with fervor.

As for Emma, she was lost in Kurt's arms.

"We did it, we did it," Billy kept repeating happily. Jay and Jake were actually dancing around the room, arm in arm.

In the glee, no one noticed that Sly had slipped to the floor, his breathing heavy and labored.

"Guys?" Sly whispered. "Guys?" No one heard him for the longest time. And then Emma turned around.

"Oh my God!" she cried, bending over the stricken drummer. The room fell silent as everyone rushed to Sly's side.

"Guys," Sly whispered weakly, "you've got . . . to call an . . . ambulance. I can't . . . breathe. . . ."

ELEVEN

Eight hours later, Sly Smith was dead.

Sly's mother and father flew in to accompany his coffin on the airplane back to Baltimore, where he was to be buried.

When Mr. and Mrs. Smith arrived on the island, grief-stricken but also relieved that their son no longer had to suffer the pain and horrible exhaustion of his disease, Billy and Carrie met them at the ferry and drove them to their room at the Sunset Inn.

Then the four of them sat on the back deck at the inn and talked. About themselves, about the band, about Sly.

Sly had loved Sunset Island so much, Billy told Sly's parents, that it would be only right to have a simple memorial service for him right there on the island before they left to go back to Baltimore, and would it be all right with them?

Sly's mother was somewhat hesitant. She wanted to bury Sly as quickly as possible, and didn't want to delay the flight. But Sly's father prevailed. So long as the memorial service didn't affect their travel plans, they'd be there with Billy.

Out of respect for Sly's family, the service was scheduled for seven-thirty in the morning of the next day, on the front lawn of the Sunset Island Community Center, whose owners had graciously agreed to lend the center for the gathering.

Emma woke up and looked around the unfamiliar room in confusion. Then she remembered where she was. She had spent the night at the Jacobses' house with Sam. Somehow knowing that she was to go to Sly's memorial service the next morning had made it too painful to spend the night alone.

Even so, Emma remembered, *I could*

barely sleep. And then I had the worst dreams. Horrible.

She looked over at Sam. Her eyes were open, too. "Hi," she said quietly.

Emma attempted a small smile. "I've never seen you voluntarily wake up this early before."

"Yeah," was all Sam replied.

"How did you sleep?" Emma asked.

"Oh, great," Sam replied. "Maybe a couple of hours at the most. You?"

"Probably less than that."

They quickly showered and dressed, Emma in a black suit, Sam in black pants and a black vest, under which was a bright pink T-shirt.

"Do you think that's really the best idea?" Emma asked hesitantly, pointing to Sam's T-shirt.

"Yes, I'm sure," Sam said defiantly. "Sly wouldn't have wanted me to wear all black. He was so full of fire, you know?"

"I know," Emma agreed. Her lip was trembling, but she willed herself to keep it together, and the two of them went downstairs.

"Good morning," Becky said quietly as Sam and Emma came into the kitchen.

"Hi," Allie greeted them.

"Morning," Dan added.

Emma looked at the Jacobses in surprise. It was six-thirty, and she had never expected that any of the Jacobses—especially Dan—would be up before her and Sam.

"Good morning, Jacobses," Sam said, going to the coffeemaker and pouring herself a cup. "What gets you guys up so early?"

"What do you think?" Becky asked. "We're coming."

"Both of us," Allie added.

"All three of us," Dan clarified.

Sam looked over at Emma with amazement.

"That's good," Emma said warmly.

"The Flirts are like our . . . Let's just say the Zits look up to them," Becky said, swallowing the last of her English muffin.

"Yeah," Allie agreed. "It's just so horrible about Sly."

"I agree," Sam said, sitting down at the table. "It *is* horrible."

Emma drank the cup of coffee Sam

handed her. Normally she never drank coffee, but it didn't matter, because she couldn't even taste it. *I'm going to hold it together,* she vowed to herself. *Sly would want me to.*

"We'd better go get dressed," Allie said to her sister. They were both still in the T-shirts and sweatpants they had slept in.

"Yeah," Becky agreed, pushing away from the table.

"Something appropriate, kids," Dan said to them.

"Dad, please!" Allie protested.

"Really," Becky agreed.

Dan shrugged, and the two girls left the kitchen to go upstairs and change.

"This wasn't my idea," Dan protested to Sam. "I couldn't stop them."

Sam shook her head. "Fine with me," she commented.

"I think it's really sweet of them to come," Emma added, sipping her black coffee.

"I'm kind of surprised that you're coming," Sam told Dan.

"It's a long story," Dan said. "The short

version is that when I was a boy, my best friend died when his mom's car was hit by a drunk driver."

"Horrible," Sam commented.

"I was eleven," Dan continued, his eyes getting a faraway look. "My parents said I couldn't go to the funeral. And I never forgave them."

Emma stared at Dan Jacobs. *Everyone has secrets,* she thought. *Everyone has a life that no one else knows about. Even Dan Jacobs.*

"I don't want my kids there alone," Dan continued. "If they want to go to the memorial service . . . I'm going to take them there myself."

"Good," Emma said in a low voice.

"It's also about AIDS," Dan said grimly.

Emma and Sam both looked at him in silence.

"I know that Becky and Allie are, well, precocious," Dan began seriously. "I see the kind of clothes they want to wear, the bikinis, the way they talk about boys all the time."

"They're growing up," Sam said tentatively.

"They're *too* grown-up," Dan said, stirring what was left of his coffee nervously. "I hope this memorial service scares the hell out of them. About AIDS."

I know what he's saying, Emma thought. *But doesn't he have any idea why the girls act like that? It seems to me that the twins are that way because of him. He's so completely inconsistent in his parenting!*

Emma sneaked a look over at Sam, who just shrugged.

I suppose this isn't the time to get into a protracted talk with Dan Jacobs about child-rearing, Emma thought. *And I'm sure he would think it's none of my business, anyway.*

Sam looked at her watch. "The service starts in a half hour. We'd better go."

"I'd like to ask you two a favor," Dan said as Sam and Emma got up from the table.

"Yeah?" Sam asked.

"I know it's a lot to ask, but . . . can the girls sit with you?"

Sam looked over at Emma. "What do you think?"

We'll be sitting with the band, Emma

thought. *But I don't see why anyone would object to having the twins sit with us.* "I think it's fine," Emma said.

"Me, too," Sam agreed. "If that's what they want."

"They will," Dan said, grinning a little bit self-deprecatingly. "They may want to go to the memorial service, but they're still my kids. And that means they won't want to be seen anywhere near their father!"

There are so many people here, Emma thought as she, Sam, and the Jacobs family walked the quarter mile or so from lower Main Street, where they'd parked, to the community center.

They'd tried to get into the parking lot at the community center itself, but there wasn't a single space to be found.

Rows and rows of folding chairs had been set up on the lawn in front of a small, makeshift wooden stage which held a podium and a microphone stand. Emma saw most everyone she knew on the island as she made her way to the front.

Everyone's here, Emma marveled. *There's*

Darcy Laken and Molly Mason! And Howie Lawrence. She gave a quick wave to her three friends, which they returned warmly. Emma could see that Darcy already had a white handkerchief in her right hand.

Getting ready, I guess. And I can't believe it . . . I even see Lorell and Diana over there.

Emma and Sam made their way to the front row, where the band and Sly's parents were to sit, and where Erin and Carrie had already saved them seats. Becky and Allie Jacobs slid in behind them, into the second row. As Dan had predicted, his daughters had no desire at all to sit near him.

"This is going to be interesting," Sam said dryly as she and Emma sat down with their friends. "Who brought tissues? Can you believe Diana showed up? I'm still ready to—"

"Save it for later," Emma interrupted her. "I brought tissues."

"Me, too," Carrie chimed in.

"Here," Carrie said to Emma and Sam, "put these on." She reached into her bag and took out a red ribbon, which Sam knew symbolized the fight against AIDS. Carrie and Erin were already wearing theirs.

Sam put hers on. "It clashes with my T-shirt, but I'll have to cope," she quipped.

Carrie grinned. "Leave it to you to think about fashion at a memorial service."

"If you can't laugh, what's the point of anything?" Sam asked.

Emma looked up at the sky. Clouds had been gathering threateningly since early that morning, and it really looked as if it was going to rain any minute now.

"I hope we don't get rained out," Carrie said, looking up at the ominous sky, too.

"That would be terrible," Emma agreed.

Billy, Pres, Jake, Jay, and Kurt walked over to the girls. They were all dressed in suits, and they looked very serious.

"Hi," Kurt said, reaching for Emma's hand.

"Hi." She moved over one seat to make room for Kurt to sit next to her.

Sam leaned her head against Pres's shoulder, and Carrie hugged Billy. No one said anything.

Finally Billy got up and slowly walked up to the podium.

The crowd, which had been buzzing quietly in soft conversation, hushed immediately when it saw Billy take his place at the podium. Billy stood there for a full ten seconds without saying anything, clearly trying to collect his thoughts.

After what seemed like an eternity, Billy cleared his throat. "I hate this," he said, his voice full of emotion. "I hate having to do this."

He looked out at the crowd, and seemed to gather some strength from the faces gazing at him.

"We're here because of Sly," Billy continued. "Sly Smith. Our drummer. My buddy."

Emma felt a lump in her throat. Without looking at her, Sam reached into Emma's lap and took a tissue.

"Some of us have a few things we want to say," Billy told the assembled mourners. "Some of us will speak it, some of us will sing it."

A distant roll of thunder boomed across the sky.

"Thanks, Sly," Billy said, a little smile crossing his face. "Thanks for the back beat. I'm glad you could make it."

The entire crowd broke into tension-dissolving laughter at Billy's joke. Sam looked over to her left at Sly's parents. Even they were laughing, though tears were rolling down Sly's mother's face.

"We're going to hear from Sly's father," Billy said, looking down at a sheet of paper, "and then from Carrie Alden. And then my partner Presley Travis and I will have something to say. Mr. Smith?"

Sly's dad stood up. Like Sly, he was small and slight, and had Sly's straight brown hair. He was dressed in a dark suit and tie. He walked to the podium, where Billy shook his hand. Then Billy sat down, and Mr. Smith was up there all alone.

"I'm Gene Smith," he said, his voice clear and unwavering. "Stuart—you knew him as Sly—was our only child. He's been gone for just two days, and already we miss him so much. . . ."

It took a moment for Mr. Smith to get a

hold of himself. Emma felt as if her heart were being wrenched from her chest.

"The last couple of years have been an ordeal for Rhonda and me," Mr. Smith finally went on. "But as bad as it has been for us, it was worse for Sly.

"He suffered a lot. He's not suffering now. That's the important thing. He's not suffering now. He's not suffering . . ."

Gene Smith's voice broke. He reached into his pocket for a handkerchief and dried his eyes.

"Sly loved this island," Gene continued, composing himself once again. "You don't know how much he loved it. All he ever wanted to do when he was away was come back."

Emma nodded. *I feel exactly the same way,* she thought. *This is a magic place.*

"And he loved the Flirts," Mr. Smith said. "Billy, Pres, Jay—you were the brothers he never had."

Emma got another lump in her throat. She looked over at Pres. His eyes were riveted on Mr. Smith, and tears streamed freely down his face. Then she looked at

Kurt, who was also weeping. She squeezed his hand.

"I only hope that, like brothers, you never forget him," Gene Smith said. "Because I promise you that Rhonda and I will never, ever forget you."

Mr. Smith was done. He nodded to the crowd, and then took his seat again. Billy resumed his place up at the microphone as a few raindrops pelted down. No one moved.

"Thank you, Mr. Smith," Billy said quietly. "We won't forget. Now Carrie Alden will speak."

Emma watched as Carrie stood up and walked to the mike. She unfolded a couple of pieces of paper and spread them out on the lectern.

"Good morning," Carrie said quietly. "I'm doing this because Billy asked me to, to speak for Sly's friends.

"I want to tell you about something that happened a few days ago," Carrie continued. "Sly had come into Lewiston, for the show up there. He asked one of us to do him a favor. It was our friend Emma Cresswell who agreed to do it."

Emma was startled to hear her name. *What was Carrie talking about?*

"Emma told me about this, and I don't think she'll mind if I share it with you this morning," Carrie continued. "Sly asked Emma to go with him to a church. Any church or synagogue. He said he didn't think God cared about what kind of church it was, so he wouldn't, either."

Emma nodded. She remembered it all so vividly.

"Emma said that Sly wanted to pray," Carrie said, holding the sheets she was reading from down on the podium against the stiff breeze that had come up. "He told Emma that he'd been praying a lot lately. He said it helped."

Carrie looked over at Emma. "Emma went in with him," she continued. "And she told me that she prayed, too. And it did help. She told me so."

Carrie looked over at Emma again. "With Emma's permission, I want to tell you all what she told me she prayed for that day."

Emma nodded, biting hard on her lower lip as tears coursed down her cheeks.

"Emma prayed for God to let Sly live for as long as he needed to," Carrie said. "Well, I feel like her prayer was answered. Sly lived long enough to see his band get a record deal. Those of you who knew him well know that was the biggest dream of his life."

An audible sob escaped from Emma's lips, and Kurt squeezed her hand again, harder this time, as if to say, "I'm with you."

"And when Sly finished praying," Carrie continued, "this is what Sly said to her." Here she managed to smile. "He said, 'Let's rock and roll.'

"That was Sly," Carrie said simply. "He was very special. And now I'd like to ask that we all take a moment to pray in our own way, and to remember Sly the way we want him to be remembered."

Carrie closed her eyes on the podium. Emma closed her eyes, too, and thought, very deeply, about the friend who was now gone, gone so young, gone because of a virus that all the scientists in the world had not yet been able to conquer.

When Emma opened her eyes, Carrie had left the podium and retaken her seat next to her. Billy and Pres were standing together on the platform, and each had his guitar.

"I'm Presley Travis," Pres said in his soft Tennessee accent. "This is a song that Billy, Sly, and I used to play together."

Billy and Pres played a short introduction, and then began a song that Sam, Emma, and Carrie all knew very, very well—an old spiritual that the band had sung many, many times together. Pres sang the first verse alone.

Sometimes I feel like a motherless child.
Sometimes I feel like a motherless child.
Sometimes I feel like a motherless child.
A long, long, long, long way from home.

Billy picked up the second verse.

Sometimes I feel like I'm almost gone.
Sometimes I feel like I'm almost gone.
Sometimes I feel like I'm almost gone.
A long, long, long, long way from home.

And then Billy and Pres did something unexpected. With a brief instrumental bridge, they segued into the lyrical opening of a popular Flirts song, "You Take My Breath Away":

> Each and every day
> You take my breath away. . . .
> What more can I say,
> You take my breath—

Before they sang the last word of the song, they went into another instrumental bridge. This time, what came out of the bridge was a patched-together verse from the Flirts song that Carrie had actually written herself, "No One Knows Love":

> So if I trust you, show you my heart,
> Will it be the end, or only the start?
> Because no one knows love the way that
> I do.
> No one knows how to play it so cool.
> So who can I trust? Where should I be?
> No one knows love, especially—

The two of them cut the verse off before the end, as if to say symbolically that the song couldn't be whole that day without Sly playing the drums. And then they segued back into the spiritual, without losing a single beat.

Sometimes I feel like a motherless child.
Sometimes I feel like a motherless child.
Sometimes I feel like a motherless child.
A long, long, long, long way from home.

Sometimes I feel like a motherless child.
Sometimes I feel like a motherless child.
Sometimes I feel like a motherless child.
A long, long, long, long way from—

Billy and Pres stopped playing. Emma held tightly to Kurt with one hand and tightly to Sam with the other. Sam had her hand linked to Carrie's, who was holding Erin's hand, which held Jake's, which held Jay's. And so they were all linked together, all grieving as one.

The memorial service was over.

TWELVE

Emma stared out at the high waves breaking on the shore, and she sighed.

It was the next morning, and Jane had kindly given Emma the morning off so she could be alone. She had come to the beach to think.

But as she stared out at the water her body was weary, her mind felt dull, and nothing seemed to make any sense to her.

How could Sly be alive one day and dead the next? she thought. *What does it all mean? And what is the point of anything if we're all going to die?*

She sighed again and let a handful of sand sift through her fingers. Then she reached down and did it again, and the falling grains felt like fragile life itself. In the distance some terns called to each other mournfully and circled lazily in the cloudy sky.

They're so free, she thought, looking up at the birds. *But they die, too. Everything dies.*

Even me.

"Emma?"

She turned around quickly.

"Kurt!"

He crouched down next to her on the towel she'd placed on the sand and looked at her intently. "You doing okay?"

"Not really," she admitted. "How did you happen to find me?"

"Jane told me she thought you went to the beach," Kurt said. "I took a guess that you'd pick this place, by the far pier. It's the most deserted." He sat down and looked out at the water.

"It's so quiet here," Emma said in a soft voice. "You could almost pray right here."

"I have," Kurt said. "Many times. You know how I feel about this island. It's like a church to me—sacred."

Emma nodded. "Sly loved it here as much as we do. And we're here, and he's gone. Why?"

"I know he loved it here," Kurt said quietly. "And why is he gone while other people commit murders and get away with it? I don't know."

They were silent for a long time.

"I just can't believe . . ." Emma began.

"I know," Kurt said again. "I felt the same way when my mom died."

Emma looked at Kurt. His mother had died from cancer when he was very young. She reached for his hand. "It doesn't make any sense, does it?" she asked gently.

He shrugged. "Not to me, anyway. Maybe to God." He stared up at the terns. "I remember my mom was so sick, and she was in so much pain, like Sly," Kurt said. "I wanted her to do something for me—read me a story or something—and she couldn't. I got so mad at her. . . ."

The birds above them cried out to each other more insistently. One swooped down to the water as Kurt and Emma watched. Then another, and then another. They were feeding on something in the water. More clouds scudded in, and the sky began to darken, just as it had the day before, at Sly's service.

"So I told her I hated her, and I ran out of her bedroom," Kurt recalled. "Right after that she went back to the hospital, and she never came home again."

"Oh, Kurt—" Emma began.

"I've always remembered that," Kurt said, seeming not to have heard her. "And I've always wished I could have just one more minute with her, to tell her how much I loved her."

"You never told me this."

"No," Kurt said. "But I'm telling you now."

"I'm so sorry," Emma said in a whisper. "You were only a little boy. . . ."

"Mmm," Kurt said reflectively. "I've forgiven myself—or tried to, anyway." He looked at Emma. "Sly knew how much we all loved him, don't you think?"

"I do," Emma agreed. She smiled. "Remember how he was dead set against the band's adding backup singers?"

Kurt nodded. "Sly was always a guy who fought for what he believed in, especially if it was about music."

"I'm so sorry he isn't going to get to be a part of this record contract."

"At least he knew it happened," Kurt said. "That meant a lot to him."

"Kurt?"

"Hmm?"

"I keep thinking," Emma began in a faltering voice. "What is the point of anything, really? I mean, everyone dies."

" 'To everything there is a season,' " Kurt said simply. " 'A time to be born, a time to die.' "

"That's from the Bible, isn't it?" Emma asked.

"Yeah," Kurt said. "And that's just the way the world is. My dad once told me that if people never died, we wouldn't really appreciate being alive. He said it was the price you paid for living."

Emma raised her eyebrows. "Your dad said that?"

"Hey, he's deeper than you think," Kurt

replied. "You should try talking to him sometime."

"Kurt—"

Kurt laughed. "I don't mean today, Emma. I mean sometime."

Emma leaned her head against Kurt's shoulder. "I don't want to die," she whispered.

He leaned down and kissed her softly. "You're going to live to be a really old lady with no teeth," he said. "And we'll be gumming our baby food together."

Emma laughed. "You think so?"

"I know so," Kurt said firmly. "And there's one thing you need to know."

"What's that?"

"I hate strained beets," Kurt confessed.

"Hey, you two!" a female voice called out from behind them.

They both turned around. Carrie, Sam, Billy, and Pres were walking toward them.

"Hi," Emma said, happy to see her friends. "What are you guys doing out here?"

"The same thing you're doing," Sam said. "We stopped by the Hewitts', and Jane said—"

"That's how I found her, too," Kurt told them.

"Great minds think alike," Sam joked.

Everyone sat down in the sand, either on or near the towel.

"I guess none of us felt like being alone this morning," Billy said, throwing a shell toward the water. It landed short of the waterline.

"I woke up this morning, and it was so weird," Sam began. "At first I felt happy, you know? I thought, 'Wow, the Flirts finally got their record deal!' And then I remembered. . . ."

"It doesn't seem real," Emma said. "I know."

"It's so unfair, man," Billy said angrily. "It's just so unfair."

"Whoever told you life was gonna be fair?" Pres asked him.

"Well, I hate it," Sam said. "It shouldn't be like this."

"It ain't up to you," Pres said.

"When did you get so philosophical about it, big guy?" Sam asked.

Pres shrugged. "What is, is. That doesn't mean I don't grieve."

"Pres and I are working on a new tune," Billy said. "For Sly. We want to put it on the first album."

"And dedicate the album to him," Pres added.

"That's great," Emma said warmly.

"I have this feeling," Billy began. "Like I want to pack all the living I can into each day or something. Because you never know. . . ."

Emma gulped hard. "If anything happened to any of you . . . I don't think I could stand it."

"Ditto," Sam mumbled. "You guys are family."

Emma thought about that a moment. *Sam is right,* she thought. *These people are my family. I guess sometimes family can be who you choose it to be.*

They were all silent for a while, each alone with their thoughts.

"You think Sly can see us right now?" Sam finally asked.

"I don't know," Kurt said.

"I believe he can," Sam said firmly.

"I thought you didn't even believe in God," Carrie pointed out.

"I'm allowed to change my mind," Sam said. She stood and stared up at the morning sky. "Hey, Sly!" she called. "How's it going?"

"You're crazy, girl," Pres said, but there was love in his voice.

"So, listen," Sam continued. "We're all down here and we're all bummed out that you're gone. Hey, do they have rock and roll where you are? I bet they do. Which means you're playing in some incredible band with a record deal that lasts more than a lifetime!"

Her friends laughed.

"And there's no Shelly Plotkin!" Sam yelled. "Or Cody Leete!"

Everyone laughed.

Sam whirled around to face her friends. "He hears me. I know he does."

"You're crazy," Billy said gruffly.

"No, I'm not," Sam maintained. "And he'd hear me even better if *you* yelled, too."

Billy just shook his head and threw another shell out toward the water.

Emma looked at Sam's defiant face, and then she too stood up. "Hey, Sly!" she called, even though she felt silly. "We miss you!"

"We miss you!" Sam and Emma called together.

And then, one by one, Kurt, Carrie, and Pres got up, too, and all of them yelled up to the sky, "Sly! We miss you!"

Carrie turned to Billy, who had tears streaming down his face. "I can't do it, man," he said.

"Yes," Carrie told him, "you can." She reached out for him, and slowly he took her hand. She pulled him to his feet. "Just look up at the sky," she told him. "Sly is up there somewhere. He hears us."

All six of them stared up at the cloudy sky. "Sly! We miss you!" they yelled as one voice. "We miss you!"

Through her tears, Emma saw the largest cloud drift away. The sun shone down on them in all its glory.

And she knew there were more than six souls listening to their voices raised in love. There were seven.

And he would always be with them.

SUNSET ISLAND MAILBOX

Dear Readers,

What a sad book, huh? I was crying at the keyboard while I was writing it, and Jeff came in and saw me. When he asked me what was wrong, I told him that Sly had just died in my book. So he sat down and read it, and he cried, too.

Remember—your actions have consequences. Viruses don't make any distinction between rich or poor, black or white, Christian or Jew, kid or adult. Do what you need to do to keep yourself safe.

On a different note, there's now another way to reach me: by e-mail. You can find me on America Online (AOL): my screen name is AuthorChik. (Thank you, Lisa Hurley! Lisa, one of your cool Sunset sisters, can be found on AOL as MissFlexi.) My Internet address is authorchik@aol.com. And there is frequently a discussion of the books you love on the Teenscene bulletin board section! I read all my e-mail and try to reply to it when there's not too much. But I still guarantee that if you write to me by snail-mail (regular mail!) every single letter will get a personal reply.

I continue to think my readers are the coolest. Have a great start to the school year, and we'll see each other in Sunset Holiday in a few months!

See you on the island!
Best-
Cherie Bennett

Cherie Bennett
c/o General Licensing Company
24 West 25th Street
New York, New York 10010

All letters printed become property of the publisher.

Dear Cherie,

I just got through reading another of your great books, Sunset Fire. *Just like the rest of your books, I had trouble putting it down! In the back you mentioned that a lot of readers suggested you write a book from a guy's point of view. I totally agree, but I also think you should write one from Diana's perspective. Keep on writing and I'll definitely keep on reading.*

Sincerely,
Lindsay Yeo
Ontario, Canada

Dear Lindsay,

Thanks for the idea. But frankly, I don't like Diana enough to write a book from her point of view! Now, someone might be able to talk me into doing one from the point of view of Pres!

Best,
Cherie

Dear Cherie,

I love reading your Sunset books. I especially like the fact that they are so realistic and related to current issues. Lately, everyone has been asking me what I want to study in college and do for a living. I have thought about becoming a writer, but I don't know if I have what it takes.

Love,
Emily Bowers
Cherry Hill, NJ

Dear Emily,

How's life in Tomato Mound, NJ? You've got plenty of time to figure out what to do with your life . . . both Jeff and I made big career changes well after college. As for becoming a writer, the thing to do is write, write, write, and write from your heart. You'll soon find out whether it's a career for you. Also consider nonfiction writing, journalism, writing reviews of plays and films, etc.

Best,
Cherie

Dear Cherie,

I love all your books, I'm now reading your 23rd book. I know there are just a few more left. The thing is, I read your books so fast I think you should have smaller print and longer books. Thanks!

Your #1 Fan,
Cara Ammaccapane
Beverly Hills, MI

Dear Cara,

I'm honored that you've read so many of my books. And I'm turning them out just as fast as I can! I don't know that smaller print or longer books is the answer. I bet you're a really fast reader. Have you read them all by now? Hey—I love the name Cara. It is so pretty.

Best,
Cherie